Ho

"Tom?" Mr. Gilliam c; son. "What's all this about a social science project?"

"Tom's the team leader for half of the project," Frank said.

"Is he now?" Tom's father looked at his son in surprise and smiled. "What's this project supposed to be about?"

"Whistle-blowers in government and industry," Phil Cohen, another student in the group, said.

"Yeah," Tom said. "I said anybody who'd do a thing like that had to have something wrong in the head. If they hate their jobs so much, why don't they just quit?"

The smile vanished from Mr. Gilliam's face. In fact, he looked as if someone had just given him a hard punch in the stomach.

"I don't suppose Tom has been able to do much work this week," he said harshly. "He wasn't allowed out during school hours. And otherwise—I suppose you'd say he was grounded."

Frank and his friends didn't even have a chance to say anything. Almost before Mr. Gilliam stopped speaking, he slammed the apartment door in their faces.

The Hardy Boys Mystery Stories

Available from MINSTREL Books and ALADDIN Paperbacks

THE HARDY BOYS®

#167
TROUBLE TIMES TWO

FRANKLIN W. DIXON

Aladdin Paperbacks
New York London Toronto Sydney Singapore

This book is a work of fiction. Any references to historical events, real people, or real locales are used fictitiously. Other names, characters, places, and incidents are the product of the author's imagination, and any resemblance to actual events or locales or persons, living or dead, is entirely coincidental.

First Aladdin Paperbacks edition May 2002
First Minstrel edition May 2001

ALADDIN PAPERBACKS
An imprint of Simon & Schuster
Children's Publishing Division
1230 Avenue of the Americas
New York, NY 10020

Printed in the U.S.A.

10 9 8 7 6

THE HARDY BOYS and THE HARDY BOYS MYSTERY STORIES are trademarks of Simon & Schuster, Inc.

ISBN 0-7434-0682-6

Contents

1 The Troublemaker

Can't fall asleep, Frank Hardy warned himself. Can't let my eyes close. The second I do that, I'm doomed.

Even as he fought, Frank was losing the battle. The world became fuzzy through Frank's brown eyes. Then it grew dark.

A slight, stinging sensation on his left cheekbone made Frank's eyes pop open.

Turning to his left, Frank saw Callie Shaw seated at the desk next to his. She had lined up half a dozen tightly wadded tiny balls of paper. Her fingers were poised behind one of them, ready to flick it at him. Callie looked annoyed as she silently moved her lips. Frank could read what she was saying: "Stay awake."

Frank tried, but everything was working against him. The classroom was too hot, and the stuffy air felt as if everyone else in class had breathed it before it got to him. As Mr. Bannerman, the social studies teacher, droned on, Frank decided he might as well have been speaking Klingon for all the sense he was making.

Frank's eyelids began sliding shut again—until another spitball brought him around.

"You'll find much more on the system of checks and balances in chapter seven of your textbook." Mr. Bannerman pushed his glasses up on his nose, a hint that his lecture was finally coming to a close. "Read that for our next class."

Frank glanced at the clock. There were still fifteen minutes before the period came to an end and lunch began. Mr. Bannerman stepped back to his desk and picked up a piece of paper. From where Frank sat, he couldn't read it. It looked like an official letter, though.

The teacher cleared his throat. "I received a cheerful announcement from the school board today," he said. "The members are pleased to announce a social science fair to be held six weeks from Saturday. All students will be expected to display projects in the school cafeteria."

Frank noticed that the students in the class looked a lot less than pleased.

Mr. Bannerman went on. "Class members may

work in teams of up to six students." He glanced around. "Perhaps you'd like to spend the rest of the period choosing partners."

Suddenly the room was bustling. Frank stood and stepped the short distance to Callie. Her blue eyes twinkled as she brushed back her blond hair. They were quickly joined by Phil Cohen, a grin on his thin, usually serious face.

"Good," Callie murmured. "At least we have *one* bright person on our team."

"Speak for yourself," Frank replied as Kevin Wylie and Liz Webling also joined their group.

In moments the class had divided itself into six teams—and one lone figure.

Tom Gilliam sat slumped in his seat, his lips twisted in the half sneer he usually wore. He glanced around at his classmates as if they were a flock of sheep unquestioningly following their shepherd.

Frank returned his look. Tom had transferred to Bayport High in the middle of the quarter, but he already had a reputation as a troublemaker. Every class had a Tom Gilliam, someone who'd mouth off to teachers and find a way to disrupt classes. Tom Gilliam took things so far, though, that he hadn't made a single friend at Bayort High. But someone had hung a mocking nickname on him that seemed likely to stick—Trouble Boy.

Mr. Bannerman stepped over to Tom, clearing

his throat again. "I see you haven't chosen a team, Mr. Gilliam."

"That's because nobody wants him." Callie hadn't meant her comment to be public, but her words came out in one of those moments of dead silence. Everyone heard, and the classroom filled with snickers and barely controlled laughter.

Frank could see that Tom had heard, too. His long, pale face went as red as his blazing hair.

Mr. Bannerman pretended nothing had happened. "Since you apparently can't make a choice, I'll do the job for you."

The teacher's eyes ranged the room, landing on Frank's team. "This group here, I think." His hand went for Tom's shoulder to steer him, but the new kid was already out of his chair, almost flinching from Mr. Bannerman's touch.

"Well, isn't this just great?" Callie muttered, keeping her voice even lower than usual.

Tom Gilliam faced the group as if he expected fists to fly. He stood uncertainly for a moment, then the sneer came back to his face.

"Since you chose teams so quickly you can take the rest of the period to discuss topics." Mr. Bannerman rustled the letter. "According to this, your project should deal with important subjects and movements of the past fifty years."

"Fifty years," Kevin Wylie repeated. "I wonder why they set up a cutoff date like that."

"Because anything before that stops being social studies and becomes ancient history," Tom Gilliam cut in.

Callie just ignored him. "So what do we do for a topic? What's a big deal in the last fifty years?"

"Decline of unions?" Frank offered.

"The decline of newspapers?" Liz suggested, topping him.

Frank had to grin. Both Liz and her dad worked for the *Bayport Gazette*.

"I think we need something a little—um—hot," Callie said.

"Like do parents have the right to block kids' access to particular Web sites on the Internet," Tom threw in.

"Maybe that's a little *too* hot," Frank said.

"So, do we want to do something with good guys and bad guys?" Callie asked. "Maybe something to do with crime?"

Kevin laughed. "Why not? We've got Mr. Detective here."

Frank became uncomfortable. "I think we should go for something different," he said. "Something nobody else would choose."

"How about protests?" Kevin suggested. "There have been a lot of those in the last fifty years."

"I bet nobody will think of that," Tom said sarcastically.

"I saw something on the Net that might tie in with that," Phil said. "This guy wrote a paper about people who protest by blowing the whistle, exposing corporate wrongdoing."

"Whistle-blowers," Callie said. "That's different."

Liz nodded. "Like that guy who ripped the lid off the whole cigarette business. Pretty cool."

Tom looked as if he'd bitten into a sandwich that had gone bad. "Come on. Guys who rat out their companies are real losers. Nutcases, or people about to lose their jobs."

Frank glanced around the group. Callie, Kevin, Liz—everybody was glaring at Tom. Frank wasn't surprised. Even he was getting tired of Tom's smart mouth.

"I like this whistle-blowing thing," Frank said.

"Me, too," Callie snapped.

"Frank, Callie, Phil . . ." Kevin said. "I think my vote gives the whistle-blowers the majority."

"And mine makes it almost unanimous," Liz added.

"I think Tom may have a point," Phil said. "So why don't we work his idea into the project? We can explore the pro–whistle-blower point of view—and the opposite."

"Yeah," Frank agreed. "Tom here can head up the anti–whistle-blower team, Phil the pro."

Tom just stood with his mouth hanging open.

For once he didn't have a word to say—nasty or otherwise.

The bell finally rang, and everybody thundered out of the classroom. Frank and Callie stuck their books in their lockers and headed for lunch. Callie was still annoyed at Tom Gilliam. "We really have to thank Mr. Bannerman for sticking us with that guy," she complained to Frank as they entered the cafeteria.

"Look at it from a teacher's point of view," Frank joked. "He wants to help Tom break out of his shell and enter the mainstream of school life."

"Breaking and entering," Callie muttered. "I bet there are lots of people who'd love to catch Gilliam doing that."

"Hey, guys," Frank's younger brother, Joe, said as he joined them in line. "What's the word?"

"I can't remember. Are you taking social studies this year?" Callie asked.

The younger Hardy brother nodded his blond head.

"Oh, are you in for happy news," Callie told him. "We have to do special projects. Actually, maybe it's only for seniors. I don't know for sure if juniors have to do it—"

Her report was interrupted by a shout from farther up the line. Then came the clatter of falling trays and plates.

Frank, Joe, and Callie all whipped around.

None of them could believe their eyes. Their jock pal, big, beefy Biff Hooper, was staggering out of the food line.

And charging him, throwing a punch at his face, was Tom Gilliam.

2 Stakeout

"We have to stop this before they get in trouble,"
Joe said. He moved to Biff, while Frank tried to
stop Tom.

Joe definitely had the easier job. Biff wasn't
even fighting. He appeared almost dazed. "What's
with that guy?" he asked. "I just made a comment
about his shirt, and he starts swinging at me."

Biff put a hand to his jaw. "I have to admit, the
guy throws a pretty good punch."

A sudden yelp from behind Joe made him turn.
Tom Gilliam had obviously been giving Frank a
tough time. The older Hardy had thrown an arm-
lock around Tom to keep him from coming at Biff.
Gilliam was still struggling and wanted to continue
the fight.

9

"Keep that up, and you're going to break something," Joe warned. "Not to mention getting nailed by Old—uh-oh."

Joe was lucky to spot Mr. Sheldrake before calling the assistant principal by the name all the students used. "Old Beady Eyes" didn't like his nickname. He also didn't like fighting at school.

"Ah, Mr. Gilliam," he said, not sounding at all surprised. "I see you don't seem to listen to your warnings. Well, you've gone well beyond the warning stage now. This school does not tolerate brawls. The school board has set very stern guidelines."

Joe watched as Frank released Tom and Mr. Sheldrake steered him toward the principal's office.

There's just no justice, Joe thought, glancing up at the sky as he headed home from the library. Tom Gilliam gets suspended from school and gets five days of beautiful weather. But when the weekend comes and *we* get off . . .

He looked again at the threatening clouds marching across the sky. The morning weather report had said nothing about rain. From the looks of things, though, Friday night was certain to be a washout.

Joe went down the block to the Hardy house and opened the door. Thanks to the clouds, very little light was coming in the windows. Joe moved through the gloomy first floor of the house, flicking on electric switches. "Anybody home?" he called out. "Or is everyone taking a nap?"

Frank appeared at the top of the stairs, silhouetted against the lights in his room. "It's just the two of us—remember? Mom and Aunt Gertrude are off setting things up for a charity auction. And Dad—"

"That's right. He's on a stakeout." Joe shot a look out the windows. "I hope they all took umbrellas."

A sudden gust of wind sent the first spatter of rain against the glass.

A sudden thunderclap sent Frank rushing to his computer. "Better turn my computer off. Just my luck for it to get fried by lightning."

The thundershower passed quickly, and the sky even cleared up for a while. Dinner was frozen Mexican food nuked in the microwave. The boys ate in the kitchen, talking about their projects.

"The terrorism thing my group chose for social sciences is turning out to be more interesting than I thought," Joe said. "Did you know that Ho Chi Minh spent several years working as a waiter in France? Then he went back to Vietnam and built the organization that threw the French out of his country, not to mention giving the U.S. of A. a big headache."

"That's what my research is giving me." Frank

sighed. "I keep finding out how whistle-blowers lose their jobs and ruin their lives. And after all their sacrifices, they still end up not making a difference." He gave Joe a lopsided grin. "Maybe I should switch over to the 'anti' side of the question with Tom Gilliam."

Joe frowned. "You of all people think folks shouldn't try to stop the bad guys?"

"Some of the stories I've found would make you wonder. I was just reading about an Australian cop who reported some of his co-workers for taking bribes. *He* was the one who got dumped off the force. Luckily, he was able to get the press interested and got some big bucks in legal damages."

"So it turned out all right," Joe said.

Frank shook his head. "Maybe all right financially, but this guy was never able to work as a cop again. And it turned out that the same corruption continued. The whistle-blower went through a lot of grief—for nothing." He sighed. "And that was one of the better stories."

"Frank, you're bumming me out," Joe said. "Cheer up! We've got a weekend ahead of us—"

He glanced out the window. The rain had started again—a steady drumming that didn't look as if it would let up soon. "As long as we don't get washed away."

The phone rang, and Joe popped up from the table to get it. "Hardy residence," he said.

"I'm glad you're in," his father's voice said over the line.

"Dad! What's up?" Joe asked.

"I'm downtown, staking out the old Harbor Hotel," Fenton Hardy replied. "This change in the weather has caught me off guard."

Wherever his dad was calling from, the raindrops were hitting him pretty hard. Joe could hear them even over the phone. "What do you need, Dad? An umbrella? Your trench coat?"

"What I really need is one of those plastic rain ponchos we picked up in the ninety-nine-cent-store," Fenton Hardy said. "Not the fluorescent orange or the baby blue. Something on the dark side, if you can manage it."

Joe remembered the rain gear his father was mentioning. They'd picked up a bunch of one-size-fits-all ponchos in a job lot store. For a joke, he'd modeled one. Frankly, he'd found thicker, stronger plastic in the better brands of garbage bags. "Are you sure?" he asked.

"It's what I need to fit in around here." Fenton gave Joe a pair of cross streets. "Pull up there, and I'll signal you."

"You're the boss," Joe said. He went down into the basement and rooted around in the "junk drawer" of his father's office. It took a little digging to locate the rain ponchos, but he did and began sorting them. Yes, there were a couple in bright orange.

"Pretty ugly," he muttered.

He turned up another poncho—this one in light green. And then pay dirt. The plastic raincoat was dark green—certainly the dingiest Joe had been able to find. The package was so small, he crammed it in his back pocket and headed up the stairs.

"Dad wants me to drop something off for him," Joe told Frank. "Could I have the keys to the van, or do you want to drive?"

Frank dug the keys out of his pocket. "You go," he said. "I'm going back on-line to try to find some happier whistle-blower stories."

Joe caught the keys, then ran upstairs for a couple of items his father might appreciate, even if he hadn't asked for them. He came back down with a small bundle, grabbed an umbrella, and went outside.

Stopping at the intersection Fenton had named, Joe peered out into the downpour. The windshield wipers were working overtime to clear a partial view. Suddenly Joe heard a knock at the rear of the van. He ran to open the back doors. Before setting off downtown, he'd already loosened the bulb in the dome light. That way, no one could see inside if the doors were opened.

Fenton Hardy quickly slipped inside, moving up to the front seats. Joe blinked when he got a look at his father in the watery illumination from the streetlights. Besides being soaking wet, his usually neat father looked—well, like a bum.

Obviously, Fenton hadn't shaved that morning. His sodden clothes weren't just old, they were threadbare. Joe wrinkled his nose. They also smelled.

Fenton gave his son a grin. "The building boom down by the waterfront hasn't reached here yet," he said.

Joe nodded. He'd noticed that the neighborhood had a pretty skeevy tone.

"The best way to keep an eye on the entrance to that house is to camp out in the alley across the street." He flapped his soaked clothes. "And who would do that?"

Joe finally understood. "A homeless person."

Fenton nodded toward a derelict brick hotel in the middle of the block. "Inside there is a well-known burglar, one Stinky Peterson. I'm betting he made a pearl necklace disappear from an apartment in the Harbor Pavilion."

The detective shook his head. "The owners trusted a necklace a quarter of the way to six figures to a wall safe that was one step up from a tin can. The insurance company would like to get the pearls back, and I think Peterson has them. Of course I can't prove it to the police."

"So you're keeping an eye on him," Joe said.

"Sooner or later, he'll have to move the goods," Fenton agreed. "If I catch him fencing them, then maybe I'll be able to bring the cops in." He glanced down at the plastic bag at his feet. "What's this?"

"A couple of things I thought you might need," Joe said. Fenton was already pulling out the towel stowed on top and began rubbing it through his dripping hair.

"There's also a T-shirt and a pair of jeans. I didn't realize you were down here in—um—disguise. Otherwise, I'd have brought your gardening clothes." Joe grinned.

"Oh, no!" Fenton exclaimed.

Following his father's gaze through the windshield, Joe saw a dark, late-model sedan pull up in front of the Harbor Hotel. A figure dashed out from the doorway through the raindrops.

"That's Peterson!" Fenton dug an infrared camera out from under his clothes. "Got to get closer if I'm going to get anything halfway clear in this rain."

Before Joe could say anything, his father had opened the door and stepped out into the rain. Fenton crept down the block in a crouch, virtually disappearing against the cars and vans he passed. Even Joe could barely spot him against the movement of the windshield wipers.

Fenton suddenly froze. Peterson was standing in

the street, leaning toward the driver's window. He had a small package in his hand as he reached in. When his hand came out, he was holding a thick envelope. Ignoring the rain, Peterson ripped the envelope open and riffled the contents. Still crouching, Fenton shot pictures of the transaction with his camera.

That was when the sport utility vehicle came around the corner, swinging wide to avoid Joe's double-parked van. As the SUV slid back into its lane, the high beams lit up Fenton.

Peterson yelled something, jumping back from the parked sedan like a scalded cat. He had nearly gotten run down by the SUV as it passed.

The sedan's engine roared to life as it began to pull away. Fenton Hardy passed behind it, camera up to catch a final shot of the license plate. But he must not have been satisfied with that. Fenton dashed across the street toward his sedan. Joe realized that his father must have stashed his car on the street before taking up his homeless disguise.

Fenton already had the remote in his hand. The car gave out a loud chirp as he unlocked the doors. He reached the street-side door—

But the driver of the escaping car must have spotted him about to take up the pursuit. The dark sedan came to a sudden halt. Then, with a screech of rubber, the car began heading back up the block—in reverse!

The big, dark car fishtailed, swerving wildly across the pavement. But there was no doubting where it was aimed.

It was heading straight for Fenton Hardy's car— or rather, for Fenton Hardy!

3 Pros—and Cons

"Dad!" Joe yelled, even though he knew his voice couldn't be heard outside the van. He was too far away to help his father, even if he threw the van into gear and floored it. In a split second, Joe tried the only thing possible. He put one hand on the horn and leaned on it with all his might, at the same time flashing his high beams.

Maybe the sudden noise or dazzling light distracted the other driver. Maybe he or she hit an oil spot. But the car backing up rapidly skidded, colliding only with the front fender of Fenton's car. Fenton had already flung himself toward the sidewalk, rolling over the hood of the car.

Joe's breath caught in his throat as the two cars came together in a splintering crunch. The attacking sedan suddenly shifted into forward again, wheels shrieking on the pavement. For a second the dark car seemed stuck. Then, with a screech of tearing metal, it pulled free and went careening down the block.

Joe tried to start his own engine, tried to turn the van to cut off the escaping car. He was a hair too late. The dark car was already past him as he swung the van around. His last view of the fence's getaway came through the rain-speckled passenger door window. The driver of the escaping car cut his turn so sharply, he took the corner on two wheels.

No chance to catch him, Joe thought bitterly. By the time I get this thing turned in the right direction, that guy will have disappeared.

Instead, he pulled the van back into a double-parked position and scanned the area for Peterson. No luck. He went to his dad.

Fenton stood beside his car, shaking his head. One look told Joe why his father hadn't set off on the fence's trail. The right front fender of the car was pushed in as if it had been hit with a giant hammer, and the wheel beneath stuck out at a crazy angle.

"I don't think this is even a job for the body shop," Fenton said, kicking the tire. "Looks to me like a broken axle."

He grinned at Joe, wiping rain off his face with

the back of his shirt sleeve. "Let's get back in your ride. No need for *both* of us to get soaked."

Fenton climbed in the passenger seat and strapped on his seat belt. He dug a cell phone from under his stained, soaking shirt and hit three digits. "Police? This is Fenton Hardy. I'm a private investigator, looking into the Nugent burglary—Yes, the pearls."

Joe listened as his father calmly described his close brush with death. "It was a late-model standard. Here's the license number." He then recited a series of letters and numbers from memory.

"Yes, I have photos of the car. I'll be at my home. For the time being, I'll leave my car where it is. There's no way I can drive it. Thank you."

He cut the connection. "The boys in blue will be looking for that car. Maybe we'll get lucky."

Joe shook his head. "I can't believe how you could just reel off the license plate, considering what just happened."

His father gave him a crooked smile. "It's amazing how the threat of death can concentrate your attention—and your memory."

"That driver was trying to kill you—squash you like a bug against your own car." Joe began to get angry. "I didn't even get a good look at him, her . . . or it." He turned to his father. "I know who did, though. That burglar, Peterson. We should find him and bring him right to the cops—"

Fenton shook his head. "Long gone by now."

"But he must have gone up to his room in the hotel. And we've been right here at the front door—" Joe began.

"This guy is a burglar, Joe. He knows how to get in and out of windows, how to use fire escapes, roofs . . . you name it."

"So you lost your pearls *and* your burglar."

Fenton shrugged. "Comes with the territory sometimes. That's not what bothers me."

"Seeing you almost get killed is what bothers *me*," Joe said as he started the van for home.

"I'm more interested in why," Fenton said. "Peterson is a professional. He'd deal only with pros. And no pro would act like such a cowboy, even over twenty-five grand's worth of pearls."

"I've heard about guys who'd kill people for less than a quarter of that amount," Joe objected.

"Apples and oranges," Fenton replied. "That's a different branch of the business. No thief would let himself get stuck with a murder rap. It brings too much attention. The cops would be all over it."

"The papers are full of people getting killed during robberies," Joe pointed out.

Again, Fenton shook his head. "Amateurs. People pulling a job for the first time, either with no plan or a bad one. When something goes wrong, they panic. That's not Stinky Peterson's kind of criminal. When he hit the Nugents' apartment at the Harbor Pavillion, he knew exactly how long they'd be away. There were no traces of a search—he went straight for the safe. Only the pearls were gone. He didn't leave a single trace for the cops to connect him with the job. That's the work of a pro."

Now it was Joe's turn to shrug. "Maybe the fence wasn't a pro. Maybe he was an errand boy who panicked."

"A scared amateur would have hauled it out of there," Fenton said. "Trying to take me out was a quick decision . . . and a cold-blooded one."

"Maybe whoever it was had a criminal record," Joe suggested. "Maybe they were afraid that if they got caught, they'd get locked up with the key thrown away."

"And what would happen if they were caught for murder?" Fenton's face creased in a puzzled frown. "We're missing something in this, Joe. I don't know what it is."

"Yet," Joe put in.

That managed to get a laugh out of his father, but Fenton was soon serious again. "There's something more than meets the eye in this whole setup."

They soon got home, and Fenton wound up throwing most of his dripping disguise directly into the trash. As he headed to the bathroom for a

23

much-needed shower, he said, "I'm glad that your mother and Gertrude aren't home yet. I'll explain it all in the morning."

When Joe came down on Saturday morning, he found his mother sitting unhappily over a cup of tea in the kitchen. His dad didn't look very cheery either. At least he was freshly shaved and wearing a new sweater and casual slacks.

"Why don't you get your brother?" Fenton said to Joe. "The three of us will go out for breakfast this morning." He glanced at his wife. "Give your mom a break and a little peace and quiet."

Joe turned and went right back upstairs. Frank was dressed and coming out of his room. "Dad's taking us out for breakfast," Joe announced. "I think Mom's a little upset about last night—maybe we should use the front door instead of the kitchen."

The boys came out of the house to find Fenton waiting beside their van.

"Where to?" Frank asked, getting behind the wheel. "There's that all-you-can-eat pancake place out on the interstate—"

Fenton obviously had a place in mind. Joe watched as he began giving directions that took them downtown.

They soon arrived at a little hole-in-the-wall coffee shop a few blocks from the municipal buildings. On a workday the place would probably be jammed with people having breakfast or looking for a doughnut and coffee to bring to the office. Saturday morning, though, the Hardys just about had the place to themselves.

Frank looked around in puzzlement. "I guess I must have passed this place before," he said. "But I think this is the first time I've ever been inside."

Joe was more direct. "Okay, Dad. Why are we sitting in a greasy spoon—ouch!" His question was interrupted by a gentle kick in the shins from Fenton as the waitress came their way.

"We're here because this place makes the best French toast in this part of the state," Fenton told them. "And you can never get in here on a workday."

He ordered French toast and coffee. The boys went for the same, although they had orange juice.

"Fresh squeezed," the waitress told them when she brought the tray of beverages.

A little while later she appeared with their breakfast—big, thick slabs of hand-sliced bread soaked in egg, fried up, and sprinkled with cinnamon.

"Pretty good," Joe admitted after chewing his first piece. He lowered his voice. "But the best in this part of the state? There has to be another reason, Dad."

Fenton's eyes went to the door as it swung open, ringing an old-fashioned bell. He smiled, and Joe now knew why his dad had rushed them into this place.

A police officer the Hardys knew well took off his uniform cap as he entered the coffee shop. "Hello, Flo," Con Riley said. "The usual, I guess."

"Coffee with cream, an apple turnover, and your favorite stool at the counter." The waitress named Flo seemed to have Con's standing order memorized.

Obviously Con is a regular at this place, Frank thought. And just as obviously, Dad knows that fact. He wanted to talk to a friendly face from the Bayport force while keeping the meeting unofficial.

"Con!" Fenton said with just the right note of surprise.

The police officer had just glanced at their table when Fenton spoke. Frank watched Con's face run through several expressions. First came a look of surprise, immediately covered with a poker face. But was there a smile behind that mask?

"Fenton," Con said. "What brings you downtown on this fine Saturday morning?"

"Just taking the boys out for breakfast," Fenton replied. Now it was Frank's turn to hide a smile. Using us for window dressing while you fish for information, he silently corrected.

"There's plenty of room at our table," Fenton went on. "Why don't you join us?"

"Why not?" Con said. "Maybe I'll even have some of that French toast."

"Now I know the world has gone upside-down," Flo said.

"I'll still have the coffee with cream, though," Con told her. He sat down with the Hardys, still hiding his smile.

"Heard you had quite an adventure last night." For a second Con became pure cop. "By the way, we found the car that almost nailed you—abandoned."

"Stolen, no doubt," Fenton said.

Con nodded. "The technical boys are going over it right now. It would be nice if they could find something we can use."

He paused. "We also went to pick up your friend Mr. Peterson. Seems he left his hotel room in a big hurry." Con's coffee arrived, and he took a sip. "I understand you have some candid snapshots of Mr. Peterson with a new friend."

"That's what almost got Dad turned into road-kill," Joe interrupted.

"Any pictures of whoever was in that car?" Con was actually leaning across the table.

Fenton shook his head. "The conditions weren't exactly the best. I couldn't get a clear image of anything behind the windshield."

27

Riley sank back into his seat. "That's a shame," he said. "We'd give a lot to get a look at the face of the new boyo in town. All the crooks are in line to sell him their loot."

He gave Fenton a long look. "They say this guy has national connections."

4 Warm Welcome

Frank couldn't help himself. "So, we've got a national syndicate of criminals moving into Bayport." His lips curled in disgust. Joe had given him the full story on what had happened the night before. "If they're such pros, why did they try to crush Dad against his car? That sounds more like a bunch of joyriding kids suddenly scared of being caught in a stolen car."

Con Riley shook his head. "For one thing, these aren't homegrown organized crime types," he said. "Don't expect them to act like the fellas you see on TV or in the movies with the homes in the suburbs. Nowadays, some of the worst, most vicious gangs come from outside this country."

"America—the land of opportunity," Frank growled.

"Yeah—opportunity to rip off anything that isn't solidly nailed down," Joe put in.

Con could only shrug. "Can't argue with you. It doesn't even help to catch these characters. Jail time looks like a vacation compared to the way they'd be treated in their own countries. They're here to make a killing, and they don't care who gets killed while they do it."

"Sounds charming," Fenton Hardy said. "What have you got on them?"

"Not much." Con made a face. "Most of our . . . usual sources aren't talking. Could be they're greedy—this new fence is offering great prices." He paused. "Or maybe they're scared. These guys play rough. You heard about the big fire downtown last week?"

"The pawnshop," Frank said.

"With the owner inside." Fenton shot a glance at Con. "That was this crew?"

"The deceased was actually running a very profitable fencing operation, and he didn't want to play by the new rules." Con lowered his voice. "Here's something you didn't hear on the news. The deceased had a dent in his skull that wasn't accidental."

"This is Bayport we're talking about," Frank protested. "You're making it sound like Chicago in those old-time gangster movies. You know, where the guys in the loud striped suits fight over who controls the North Side."

"Even wise guys don't wear pinstripes anymore," Con Riley said. "The last mobster I saw was in a purple jogging suit."

"One hundred percent silk, I suppose," Fenton Hardy joked.

Con Riley wasn't laughing. "These clowns stand to rake in a lot of money if they make this thing work," he said. "And once they prove they can move whatever they steal, our local street crooks will get a lot more active."

He glanced at Fenton. "You'll probably end up doing more insurance work."

The boys' father was very serious now. "I started out as a cop," he reminded Con. "So I know what it means when street punks 'get active.' " He shook his head. "That's not the way I want my business to grow."

Fenton's eyes narrowed in thought. "The big selling point for this new fence is his promise to move the local thieves' loot out of town. Find the pipeline, and you could easily shut these newcomers down."

"*If* we can find the pipeline." Con looked as if Fenton had jabbed a sore tooth. "We've been looking and found exactly zip. Maybe this business is still too small-scale for shipments to turn up."

He sighed. "Either that, or they've got the sort of machine you see on those sci-fi shows. You know, they're beaming the stuff out."

The waitress arrived with Con's breakfast, and he stopped talking. But as he pushed the food around on his plate, it was obvious he'd lost his appetite.

I bet Chief Collig is putting on a full-court press to nail these guys, Frank thought. Not having anything to show for all this effort has to hurt.

Con's mood affected everyone at the table. They finished their meal in silence, except for the waitress scolding Con for wasting food.

Then they went their separate ways.

That afternoon Frank was working at his computer when Joe stuck his head in the doorway. "You've been hunched over the keyboard since we came home. What's up?"

Frank looked up from the computer screen and stretched. "More stuff for my social studies fair project. I stumbled across a reference to qui tam cases."

"Who's that?" Joe asked. "Some Chinese whistle-blower?"

"It's part of a Latin phrase. Old-time law is full of this stuff." Frank read from the screen. " '*Qui tam pro domino rege quam pro se ipso in hoc parte sequitur.*' "

"Oh, that makes it perfectly clear," Joe said, "if I were Julius Caesar. Why not explain it in English this time?"

"The straight translation would be 'Who as well as for the king as for himself sues in this matter.' "

Joe shook his head. "It's English, but it doesn't seem to be helping."

Frank laughed. "Tell me about it! It seems to be an old-time legal principle. Some members of congress picked it up a while back and made it part of a federal law to fight fraud. It allows private citizens to file federal lawsuits against government contractors who are ripping off the taxpayers. The idea was to go after military contractors who were selling hammers to the army at six hundred dollars a pop. But suits were filed for other agencies— even NASA—nailing companies for as much as a hundred and fifty million dollars."

"That's a lot of hammers," Joe said. "But I don't see how this stuff ties into your project."

"The law became a strong weapon for whistle-blowers. Of course, a lot of companies didn't like it. Their lawyers have been arguing that the whole concept is unconstitutional."

Joe shook his head. "Yeah, people get real patriotic when they're caught with their hands in the cookie jar."

The phone rang, and Frank picked it up. He

recognized the voice on the other end immediately. It was Kevin Wylie.

"How's it going, Frank?"

"You don't really expect me to answer that, do you?" Frank replied with a grin. "After all, you're on the other side in this project."

He expected at least a chuckle from the other boy. Instead, he got a second of dead silence. Then Kevin said, "That's sort of why I'm calling. You know that Tom Gilliam was suspended from school."

Tell me about it, Frank thought. Classes have been peaceful and quiet this past week.

"But he's supposed to be the captain of our side in this project," Kevin went on. "I suspect he hasn't done a thing. And I certainly haven't heard from him."

"Neither has Callie—not that she's complaining," Frank said.

After the captains had been named, the other kids drew lots to fill out the teams. Phil wrote "pro" on two pieces of paper, "anti" on two more. The papers were folded and shaken up in an empty book bag. Frank and Liz Webling had pulled the pro tickets. Callie and Kev wound up on the other side.

Liz was happy—she believed that whistle-blowers were important news sources. Kevin felt that whistle-blowers hurt businesses—like the one his father owned. So he was pleased with his choice, although Frank suspected he'd have liked being captain even more.

While Frank leaned toward the pro side, he realized he didn't know much about the subject. This project would be a chance to learn something.

The only unhappy person was Callie. She didn't give a hoot one way or the other on the whistle-blower question, but she had very clear—and negative—ideas about Tom Gilliam. And now she wasn't able to work with Frank.

"Look, Frank, I know you set Tom up as the team leader for a goof. But I don't think it's fair to let him drag our whole team down," Kevin complained.

"Hey, chill out," Frank replied. "It's not as though we're getting graded on this."

"I don't like people making me look bad." Frank was surprised at the angry tone in Kevin's voice.

"Have you talked to Tom about this?"

"I tried calling him on Thursday," Kevin said. "He just blew me off."

Frank sighed. "So what do you think I can do?"

Kevin hesitated for a second. "It's a little complicated. You see, Tom's father works for my dad."

Kevin's status in school had soared with his dad's business success. When Don Wylie had taken over Tri-State Express, it had been a glorified messenger service. Now the shipping company was booming, hiring lots of people—including Tom's father.

Frank realized that Kevin was trapped in a no-win situation. If he pushed things with Tom and Tom skunked him, Kevin would look foolish. On the other hand, he could go at it through his dad to Tom's father. But then Kevin would look as though he couldn't handle his own problems.

"Tell you what," Frank finally said after a moment's thought. "Callie and I were going to catch a movie tonight. Suppose I call Phil and Liz and invite them along. We could all drop by Tom's house on the way to the movies. How's that sound?"

"At least we'd be doing something," Kevin said.

You're welcome, Frank silently replied. "Let's meet at my house—say, seven o'clock?"

The Hardys had a full van as they pulled away that evening. Joe and Iola Morton were coming to the movies as well, so there were seven people on board.

Callie was not in a forgiving mood. "If Tom isn't pulling his weight, why not kick him off our team?"

"Or at least, don't make him captain," Kevin put in.

Seated up front, where Joe was driving, Frank

36

shook his head. "Mr. Bannerman stuck us with Tom. I don't think he'll let us dump him."

The Gilliams lived in an apartment building toward the center of town.

"Looks pretty nice," Liz said.

"What were you expecting?" Phil asked with a grin. "Broken windows? Street gangs?"

Joe was lucky enough to find a parking space right in front of the building. The kids piled out and went into the lobby. The door was locked, but there was a buzzer system. Frank found "Gilliam" on a fresh slip of paper beside one button and pressed it.

The voice on the other end seemed surprised that Tom had visitors. "We're classmates," Frank explained, "working on a project with him."

A second later a harsh buzz filled the lobby, and the door opened at Frank's push. He led the way to the elevator. "The apartment's on the third floor," he said.

When the elevator arrived on the third floor, Frank saw that one of the apartment doors was open. A tall, thin, stoop-shouldered man with thinning hair stood in the doorway. His gray eyes gave the kids a careful once-over as they approached. "I'm Russ Gilliam, Tom's father," he said.

Frank took care of the introductions and started in on an explanation. "We were on our way to the movies this evening. And, since we, um, hadn't seen Tom this week, we thought we'd stop by to see how he was getting along on our project."

"This is the first time I've heard about this project," Mr. Gilliam said. "Tom?" he called over his shoulder.

Tom Gilliam slouched his way to the door. "So, the gang's all here." He grinned at Joe and Iola. "With reinforcements."

"So what's all this about a social science fair and a project?" Russ Gilliam asked.

"He's the team leader for half of the project," Frank added.

Tom's father looked at his son in surprise. "Is he, now?"

Tom only shrugged. "No biggie," he said. "They were talking about topics, I gave my opinion, and all of a sudden I was a team captain."

Russ Gilliam smiled, glancing from his son to the rest of the kids. "I'm glad to hear that," he said. "What's this project supposed to be about?"

"Whistle-blowers in government and industry," Phil said.

"Yeah," Tom went on. "I said anybody who'd do a thing like that had to have something wrong in the head. If they hate their jobs so much, why don't they just quit?"

The smile vanished from Mr. Gilliam's face. In fact, he looked as if someone had just given him a hard punch in the stomach.

"I don't suppose Tom has been able to do much work this week," he said harshly. "He wasn't allowed out during school hours. And otherwise—I suppose you'd say he was grounded."

House arrest. The words seemed to pop into Frank's mind.

"So I guess there's nothing for you to discuss right now." Tom's father looked grim as he started shutting the door. "I'm sure you can talk when Tom comes back to class on Monday."

Frank and his friends didn't even have a chance to say anything. Almost before Mr. Gilliam stopped speaking, the apartment door was slammed in their faces.

5 Better than a Movie

Joe Hardy had to fight back laughter as he looked at the stunned faces around him.

"Well," he said, "now we know where Tom gets his pleasant, easygoing personality."

"Maybe weirdness does run in families," Callie said. "Or just plain rudeness."

Phil Cohen shook his head. "I don't understand it. At first Mr. Gilliam seemed a little worried."

"Wouldn't you if a delegation of people came to your home about your son?" Kevin Wylie said.

"Knowing Tom, it probably wasn't the first time that's happened," Callie put in.

"That's not what I mean," Phil said. "He was sort of wary at first. But when he started talking to us,

Mr. Gilliam sounded nice enough." Phil pressed the elevator button.

"Until his charming son came along," Callie said.

Joe glanced back at the Gilliam apartment. Loud voices filtered through the door. He couldn't make out any words, but the angry tones couldn't be mistaken. "Seems like Trouble Boy gets on everybody's nerves—even his family's."

The kids piled into the elevator and rode it down to the lobby. Outside the building, Phil looked up as if he were trying to spot the Gilliams' window. "I don't know if it was Tom so much as our topic that got Mr. Gilliam going," he muttered.

"I think anything could have set him off," Kevin Wylie said. "Did you see the look on his face when Frank introduced me?"

"I think that'd be the same look anybody would get when the boss's son turns up at your door." Liz Webling laughed.

Frank had already reached the van and was unlocking the doors. "Let's get it in gear, folks. The movies wait for no man—or woman."

"Speaking of which," Iola said as she climbed aboard, "what are we seeing?"

That started an argument as everyone found their seats. Callie mentioned *Lost Love,* a date movie. Of course, Iola and Liz cast their votes with her. Joe pushed for a film with a lot of car chases and explosions. Kevin enthusiastically backed that idea.

Phil came out with the title of some foreign film that nobody knew. Joe looked expectantly at Frank, who glanced over at Callie.

Then, to Joe's horror, his brother went along with the girls.

"*Lost Love?*" Joe said in disgust. "I can't believe you'd wimp out."

Kevin chuckled. "Maybe he was afraid of some lost love of his own if he didn't go along with Callie."

Frank cleared his throat, sounding embarrassed. "I checked the schedule before we left. *Lost Love* is the next film to start at the multiplex."

"Can't we come up with a compromise movie?" Phil suggested. "How about a good mystery?"

No sooner did he speak than the building's door flew open. Russell Gilliam came storming out. He stalked down the block to a battered old compact car. It was painted a sort of bridle path tan—where the body wasn't rusted. Mr. Gilliam got in and tried to start the car. The engine sputtered and died. From where he was sitting, Joe saw the man clench his fists and hammer the steering wheel.

Looks like nobody in the Gilliam family is easy to get along with, Joe thought.

Gilliam finally got the car's engine going and pulled away with a squeal of worn tires.

"How about a real-life mystery?" Joe asked starting up the van. He let another car pass, then swung out into traffic. "Rule number one in maintaining a tail. Don't park yourself right on the subject's back bumper. That makes it too easy to get spotted."

"What's the big deal?" Iola asked. "I don't see much of a mystery here."

"When we turned up, Mr. Gilliam was dressed for a quiet night at home," Joe said. "Sweat pants, slippers, no socks. Then he changed his clothes and went whipping out of the house."

Ahead of them, the tan compact cut off another car, a shrill whine coming from its engine. "Wherever he's going, he seems to be in a hurry," Joe added.

"Or he's out working off a bad mood with bad driving," Frank put in. "Too many people do that, you know."

Russ Gilliam screeched through a turn onto a major road. Joe swung round, his speed much slower. He was barely keeping the other car in sight. The traffic was heavier here. He let another car get between the van and the compact.

"Where's he heading at this time of night?" Liz asked.

Joe grinned. Typical reporter's curiosity, he thought.

"Could be anywhere," Callie spoke up. Her tone

43

suddenly sounded suspicious. "Maybe he just discovered they'd run out of milk." She glared at Joe. "Why are we wasting time with this silliness? What about our movie?"

"Well, if he's going on a milk run, he's heading downtown to get it," Phil said. Ahead of them, Gilliam made another turn.

"This is a shortcut my dad takes to get to our warehouse." Kevin leaned forward in his seat, peering through the windshield. "There's a street in here that angles off toward Harborside Drive. If he takes that, we'll know for certain."

Without signaling, Gilliam took the cutoff Kev had mentioned. Joe swung around more slowly. There was no traffic to offer cover. They were heading for the Bayport docks. The area was being rebuilt with condos facing the bay, but this neighborhood was still full of rundown old warehouses.

The place was also a maze of side streets, loading docks, and back alleys. When the expensive apartments, shops, and restaurants came in, people would call it quaint. Bumping through potholes on shadowy streets with few lights, Joe called it tricky.

"Time to tighten our tail a little," he announced. "It's the only way to keep our friend in sight."

He pulled a little closer on turns, but dropped back on the straightaway, trying to vary his speed so Gilliam wouldn't realize that the headlights in his mirror belonged to the same vehicle.

At last Gilliam made a final turn. A full block was taken up by a warehouse with a newly-painted sign: Tri-State Express. The red letters gleamed under the glare of the arc light that illuminated the whole front of the building.

Russ Gilliam's rust-pitted compact coasted to a stop across the street from the warehouse, near the far corner of the block.

Joe didn't make the turn. He killed the van's lights and backed up to the curb, positioning the vehicle carefully. From the driver's and front passenger's seats, they could still keep an eye on Gilliam's car. And, of course, its driver.

"Not much of a mystery." Callie's voice was sharper now. "Tom's dad had to stop off at work to take care of something."

"Right—on a Saturday night," Joe responded. "He just got dressed and whipped down to the office."

Frowning, he continued to watch the beat-up old car. "We have a new mystery now. What is our friend over there waiting for? That's obviously what he's doing."

"Maybe he dropped his keys," Iola suggested, moving up to peer out the window.

"That might explain why he's scrunched down," Joe said. "But why doesn't he open his door and get some light on the subject? Nah. He's sitting, watching, and keeping a low profile."

Russ Gilliam sat slouched in his car for several more minutes. Then the kids got to see what he was waiting for. The warehouse door swung open, and a paunchy guy in a blue uniform coat stepped out.

The guard glanced to the left, then to the right. Finally, he started walking—slowly—up the block, away from the van full of kids. With each step the security guy tapped a big, five-cell flashlight against his right leg.

Joe suddenly realized he knew this person. He'd seen him around the Bayport Police Station sometimes, during visits to Con Riley or Chief Collig. The guy was a cop, though not in Con Riley's league.

A retired cop, Joe corrected himself, taking in the unkept gray hair sticking out from under the guard's cap.

"I know your dad's company has grown by leaps and bounds lately," Frank said to Kevin. "But"—he struggled to put the words tactfully—"I think he'd better pay a little more attention to his security system."

Joe grinned. Since the present one is barely a step up from a night watchman called Pops, he added silently.

The security man finally reached the corner of

the building. He went around it, disappearing from sight. Obviously, it was part of his routine to make a complete circle of the warehouse. And just as obviously, this was the opportunity Russ Gilliam had been awaiting.

As soon as the guard was well down the next leg of his circuit, the compact's driver-side door swung open. Russ Gilliam sprinted across the street, one hand in his pocket. He headed for a smaller door set almost in the corner of the building. A second to fumble at the lock, and then he was inside.

Raising his eyebrows, Joe turned from his seat behind the steering wheel. He glanced from Kevin Wylie to Phil Cohen.

"Maybe you're going to get your wish after all, Phil," Joe said. "Okay, it's not a movie we can all agree on. But here in real life it looks like some funny business is going on here. I think we really do have a mystery on our hands."

6 Unexpected Results

There are days, Frank thought, when I wish my kid brother didn't have such a big mouth.

Joe was obviously out to provoke a response from Phil or Kevin.

Instead, he got it from Callie.

"Come off it, Hardy," she growled. "There's no mystery here. You got outvoted on what movie to see. So you're just wasting time, until it's too late for *Lost Love*."

Joe smirked. "I'm shocked, *shocked* that you'd think I could do such a thing," he said. "This is serious business. We've got a man making a stealthy entrance into a building full of valuable stuff. Not to mention that he's sneaking around after business hours."

"Actually, that's the door to the office," Kevin put in.

"Whatever," Joe replied. "Gilliam waited until the security guard was on his rounds before he made his move. Wouldn't you call that suspicious? Who knows what he's getting up to in there?"

"Mr. Gilliam was hired as an accountant," Kevin said slowly.

"So what do you think he's doing? A little late-night bookkeeping?" Joe began pushing his door open. "Maybe we ought to go in there and have a look-see."

Frank sighed. "Joe." He put a warning tone into his voice.

"What?" Joe asked, his face the picture of innocence.

"Stop making a big deal out of this," Callie said. "Most of the people here are too embarrassed to tell you, but you're acting like a—"

"I don't think we need to disturb Mr. Gilliam," Kevin quickly broke in. "If he's doing work on his own time, it's no business of ours." He took a deep breath. "I'll leave it to my dad."

Joe sank back in his seat, closed the door, and snapped the seat belt in place around his waist. "Well, I guess that's all settled." Then he turned to Frank. "So how are we doing on time? Can we still make that heart-flopper romance Callie wants to see?"

Frank checked his watch. "It started about five minutes ago," he announced.

A broad smile crept across Joe's lips. "So I guess we'll just have to see the boom-boom flick I suggested," he said smugly.

Frank shook his head. "Actually, that started half an hour ago." He grinned. "But we could still make that foreign film Phil was talking about."

Joe was mumbling to himself all the way to the Bayport Mall Multiplex. Callie was doing a slow burn. The rest of the kids exchanged amused glances over the way Joe's clever plan had blown up in his face.

To be honest, Frank wasn't too sure about the film Phil wanted to see. But if it helped teach Joe a lesson . . .

Actually, the foreign film turned out to be a pretty funny comedy. Even Callie was in a good mood by the end.

"Why can't we see American actors making films like that?" Iola asked as the group headed across the parking lot to the van.

"Oh, you will," Liz predicted. "I expect a Hollywood remake will hit the theaters next year by holiday time."

"But we'll be able to say we saw the original." Phil looked happy. For once his suggestion had been taken. Frank realized this was a rare victory for his more intellectual friend. Usually Phil got outvoted in the choice for a Saturday night movie.

We'll have to change that, Frank promised himself. Maybe I can throw my vote his way a little more often.

At least Joe wasn't a sore loser. He played bus driver for everyone in the van, delivering each kid to his or her home. It was getting pretty late by the time Joe steered on to the Hardys' street.

Frank unsnapped his seat belt and was out the door as soon as his brother parked the van. Joe slipped more slowly from behind the wheel. He stretched until Frank heard joints popping.

"Whoa! I'm bushed!" Joe announced.

"It's all that extra driving you did," Frank replied.

Joe looked hurt. "You think I'd let people bus it or walk home at this time of night?"

"I'm talking about the extra driving you did *before* the movie. That little mystery you created."

Joe shrugged. "That was then, this is now," he said. "The only mystery left is whether I have enough energy for a midnight snack. Or should I just hit the hay immediately?"

Frank snorted. "That's no mystery," he said. "You always have enough energy for a snack." He followed Joe into the house. But instead of joining his brother in the kitchen, Frank headed upstairs to his room.

Joe poked his head inside the doorway a few

minutes later. He had a chicken leg in one hand and a glass of milk in the other. "If I'd known I wouldn't have to compete with you for it, I'd have scarfed the other leg."

He took a big bite, then tried to peer at Frank's monitor. "What's up? You get another inspiration to research sun tan, or whatever it was?"

"Qui tam," Frank answered, most of his attention still on his computer. "And this research is on something completely different. I call it Bad Dad." He looked over at Joe. "Also known as Russell Gilliam."

"Remind me never to slam a door in your face," Joe said with a laugh. "So, what's the scoop on Tom's dad?"

"He sure moves around a lot," Frank said. "I used some tricks of Dad's to access part of Gilliam's credit records. His address keeps changing—a new town every three or four months. Not to mention a new job."

Joe's eyes sparkled. "Is he like that famous impersonator guy? A brain surgeon one week, a prison warden the next?"

Frank shook his head. "Nothing so exotic. Mr. Gilliam is always an accountant—but for different companies. Before he went to work for Tri-State Express, he did the books for a ball bearing manufacturer. Before that, he was working for a car rental outfit." Tapping a key, Frank kept scrolling through screen after screen. "Electrical equipment. A toy store chain . . ." Frank blinked. "An Indian casino?"

He swung round to look at Joe. "Do you see any sort of career path in that mess of jobs?"

Joe shrugged. "Maybe I was right about Tom's lousy personality being inherited. Looks like Russ lands a job, annoys everybody, and gets fired. Then he moves off to a new town and a new gig."

He stopped, struck by a new thought. "You know, there's another reason for Tom's bad attitude—he's always the new kid in town. That's got to grow old pretty fast."

Joe laughed, but Frank didn't join in. Instead, he frowned at his computer screen.

"I'll say it again—what's the deal, big brother? You didn't take the little act I pulled down by the warehouse seriously, did you? 'What's that wicked man doing in there?' "

"I'm beginning to wonder what he's doing in Bayport," Frank answered slowly.

"Working his bookkeeping buns off for Kev Wylie's father—if tonight is any example," Joe hooted.

"Short-term jobs—moving around a lot," Frank said. "What does that sound like to you?"

Joe gave his brother a what-kind-of-answer-are-you-expecting? look. Then he shrugged. "It may not be the nicest thing to say about a person.

But what that pattern says to me is . . . 'loser.'"

"I take your point," Frank said. "So, why, when I look at it, do I think, 'great cover story!'"

"Of course!" Joe broke into laughter again. "Tom's dad is a freelance secret agent! He takes his son along so no one will suspect!" He put up a finger, coming up with a new idea. "Or maybe he's one of those people in the witness protection plan. I hear that ex-mobsters sometimes have trouble settling into their new lives."

"That's a little closer," Frank said. "Except our Mr. Gilliam may be more current than ex."

"I was kidding!" Joe protested.

"Then think about this. Whenever an organization has to organize a new territory, the same thing happens. It doesn't matter if it's an insurance company or a crime syndicate. They have to send along an official representative—a front man."

Frank's dark eyes were very serious as he looked up at his brother. "What if Tom's much-traveled dad is a mob front man? Suppose he's the new fence in town?"

7 Where There's Smoke . . .

Frank watched his brother's jaw drop at his off-the-wall suggestion. "Are you serious?" Joe demanded.

Silently, Frank nodded in reply.

Joe burst into laughter. "Obviously, I'm not the only one around here who's bushed," he said. "I think you sprained your brain on this one, Frank. Stick to Qui Tam. Or better yet, go to bed."

Frank really tried to go to sleep. But his weird notion kept him tossing and turning between the sheets. Could the man they'd met tonight have burned down that pawnshop with its owner inside? Hard to tell on the basis of a few looks, a couple of words, and a slammed door.

Actually those thoughts weren't what was keeping him awake, Frank had to admit. He knew he was circling around the really disturbing question. Had Tom's father been behind the wheel of the car that had almost smeared Frank's dad?

More than ever, Frank wished that the infrared photos Fenton had taken came out. Unfortunately, they only showed a ghostly silhouette behind the windshield of the sedan. By luck—or with extreme caution—the driver had never shown himself.

Frank found himself staring at his bedroom ceiling in the predawn dimness. The shadows seemed to rearrange themselves into the front of a car. There was the windshield, there was the steering wheel . . . and behind it was Russell Gilliam. With his thinning hair and stooped shoulders, he didn't look like a gangster. But his expression was frozen in the same grim lines Frank had seen just before Gilliam shut the door in their faces.

Fantasy or reality? At this point Frank was too tired to care. But, he promised himself, I'll pass my nutty idea along to Dad. Maybe he can make something out of it.

When Frank went down to breakfast the next morning, Joe was already at the table. "Some brother you are," he accused. "First you side with Callie instead of me on the film question. Then you go along with Phil and make me look like an idiot."

"That didn't take much work," Frank replied.

Joe pretended he hadn't heard. "But worst of all you throw that little hand grenade of an idea in my lap right before I *try* to get some sleep."

The way Joe said "try" made it clear that he hadn't succeeded. "Every time I began to doze off, I saw Russell Gilliam trying to smash into Dad."

"So it's not so funny now, is it?" Frank fought back a yawn.

As if in answer, Joe's mouth gaped even wider. "Funny or crazy, I think maybe you should tell Dad."

"Tell me what?" Fenton Hardy asked, coming into the room. "You didn't put a dent in your van last night, did you?"

"No," Joe said. "We met Tom Gilliam's dad last night."

Fenton thought for a moment. "He's the kid you pegged for a troublemaker, right? The one who duked it out with Biff Hooper."

Frank nodded. "We'd like you to listen to what happened." He took a deep breath. "And what happened afterward."

As Fenton sat down, Frank tried to give a word-for-word account of what had happened at the Gilliams' door. Joe interrupted to add a few details. Then he went on to describe the way they'd seen Tom's father sneaking into the offices of Tri-State Express.

Fenton nodded. "Odd," he said, "but I don't see—"

"That's not all." Frank went on to describe his late-night computer research, ending with the theory that had kept both boys up all night.

"I don't like hunches," Frank finished. "But I can't shake the feeling that *something* is fishy about Russell Gilliam. Maybe it's the way he keeps pulling up roots and jumping into new jobs. And this latest one—a shipping company—"

He threw out his arms. "It all makes a weird sort of sense. Con Riley said the cops can't find the new fence's loot pipeline. Maybe that's because it's a legitimate company that ships packages all over the country."

Fenton frowned, his eyes intent. "I see what you mean—it does make sense in a bizarre sort of way. We suspect Bayport has been infiltrated by a gang with national connections. They would certainly need a front man to come in to organize things. In some ways this Russell Gilliam might fill the bill.

"But you've built a tall tower of guesswork on very few facts," he cautioned. "The word is that this gang is supposed to be foreign-based. But Russ Gilliam and his son seem pretty American."

"What if he had a family connection?" Frank argued.

Joe grinned. "Or maybe the gang is an equal opportunity employer."

"Most likely that's an inconvenient fact that demolishes your whole theory." Fenton got up. "Right now we can't tell one way or the other—not until we know a lot more about Russell Gilliam. So guess what just got on my list of things to do this week?"

Mr. Hardy spent a good part of the day on his computer, checking what he could on Russell Gilliam. But Frank knew most of his background check would have to wait till Monday, which was when Fenton would be able to work his professional contacts. When Frank and Joe left for school the next morning, their dad was already on the phone.

Monday also marked Tom Gilliam's return to Bayport High. Frank noticed that there wasn't a brass band on the school lawn to greet Trouble Boy. And when Frank bumped into Liz Webling between classes, she was full of Gilliam gossip.

"We both have math first period," Liz said. "Tom mouthed off to Mr. Fielding almost as soon as class started."

She shook her head. "I guess being suspended didn't adjust his attitude."

"Did you expect it to?" Frank asked. "He pops Biff Hooper in the face and gets a one-week vacation. Some minds could see that as a reward instead of a punishment."

"But think of what he's got to face coming back," Liz said. "Mr. Sheldrake is sure to have him on his hit list. And all the other kids—"

"If anybody gives him a hard time, Tom can just take a swing. Then he'll get another week off." Frank took a deep breath. "I'm sure the next discussion on our fair project will be a circus and a half."

Frank's prediction came true even sooner than he thought Mr. Bannerman set aside the last five minutes of class for the teams to discuss their progress. The members of the whistle-blower project hadn't even gotten together before Kevin was on Tom Gilliam's case.

"You can't shut us out this time," Kevin said. "Why don't you tell us what you have—or haven't—done."

"I *haven't* done much, so far," Tom admitted. "I wasn't supposed to be out during school hours. And otherwise, I was grounded."

He glared at Kevin and Frank. "Unlike some people, my dad can't afford a bells-and-whistles computer for me to surf the Net."

"Probably afraid of what you'd find out there," Callie muttered.

Tom's ears went pink, but he pretended not to hear.

Kevin paid no attention. He was still busy dumping on Tom. "Excuses get no work done,"

Kevin said. "We're all taking this project seriously. You're supposed to be responsible for half the presentation—"

"If this is about being captain, Wylie, I know Frank made me a captain to shut me up. Do you have a new nickname for me now—Captain Trouble Boy," he said angrily.

"I just want you to do some kind of work besides moving your mouth." Kevin looked around at the other members, expecting their support.

The problem with Kevin is that he never knows when to stop, Frank thought.

The buzzer blared over the PA system, and kids grabbed their books and began trooping out.

Joe caught up with Frank at the cafeteria. "So, what's the latest chapter in the high school soap opera of Tom Gilliam aka Trouble Boy?" he asked with a grin.

"Kev Wylie kept mouthing off to him—generally about the way Tom keeps mouthing off." Frank shook his head. "We're lucky the period ended, otherwise—"

"I'm talking to you, Gilliam!" Kevin Wylie's shrill voice cut through the cafeteria noise. "You've got to shape up—I'm not going to carry you!"

Frank turned to where the shouting was coming from. Kids were moving out of the way, heading for spots where they could watch the expected fight.

"Old Kev's really pushing it, isn't he?" Joe muttered. "Does he think he's got a stronger chin than Biff Hooper?" Frank watched Tom Gilliam as Kevin kept up his tirade. But Trouble Boy didn't explode. He clenched his fists and grit his teeth but didn't take a swing.

"Of course," Frank said quietly to Joe, "Kev's dad is Tom's father's boss. If he slugs Kev to shut him up, Tom could cost Mr. Gilliam his job."

Or maybe, Frank thought, Tom knows his father will get really nasty if Tom fouls things up with Tri-State Express.

The other kids got bored quickly when it became obvious there wasn't going to be a fight. Finally, Kevin shut his mouth and began feeding his face.

The rest of the day at school passed without any more incidents. When the Hardy brothers got home, Frank immediately headed for Fenton's basement office. "How's the background check on Russell Gilliam going?" he asked.

His dad pointed to the computer screen. "I don't have everything yet, but I've assembled enough to paint a very interesting picture."

Fenton ran the display backward. "Here's the basic facts—birthday, schooling, et cetera. Gilliam was your basic middle-American, middle-class, boring kid." He glanced over at Frank. "No hint of any foreign connections in his family."

The display rolled on. "Young Russ graduated with an accounting degree, went to work for a middle-size firm, got certified, married, and became a father. Then he switched jobs, becoming a middle manager for a government program. That's when things began to change."

Frank leaned forward. "Change how?"

"He held this job for less than a year, leaving very suddenly." Fenton shook his head. "Something shady went on there—I haven't been able to find out exactly what. But it certainly had an effect on Gilliam's family. His wife sued for divorce, getting custody of young Tom. Ever since, Russ Gilliam has kept on the move, all over the country. As you found out, his employment record has been, well, spotty. Gilliam seems to hold on to a job for only a couple of months. But he doesn't clear out in disgrace. Often he leaves with a golden handshake."

Frank blinked. "A what?"

"A very generous farewell check—the sort of thing that usually goes to an important executive." Fenton frowned. "But he seems to hold only grunt jobs. There's something very wrong with this picture."

Frank looked at Joe, who'd been standing in the doorway, eavesdropping. His brother had the same worried expression that must be on his own face. Maybe Russ Gilliam wasn't the front man for a

63

national mob, but he seemed to be running some sort of scam. And it involved the company that a friend's father had worked hard to build up.

Fenton's digging had, unfortunately, created many more questions than answers.

There was one that troubled Frank more than the others.

What was Mr. Gilliam up to at Tri-State Express?

8 Two for the Executioner's Block

Joe couldn't believe what he found when he got to school the next morning. Everybody was talking about the run-in the day before between Kevin and Tom. Now everyone was acting as if there were going to be some sort of shootout at high noon.

Kevin was strutting around as the kids waited for the doors to open. "Trouble Boy doesn't look so tough now," Kevin boasted. "All we needed was for somebody to stand up to him."

"Aren't you afraid Gilliam might try to get even somehow?" a sophomore breathlessly asked. He glanced over to where Tom was leaning against a chain-link fence. "I mean, he could set it up as an 'accident' or a prank—something like that."

Kevin responded with a superior grin. "I'm going to keep him too busy worrying about *me*. See what I, um, borrowed today."

He reached into his knapsack, digging among its contents, and came out with something that looked like a tiny knife with a dull gray metal sheath. "My dad and I go hiking sometimes. He thinks this gadget is primo for starting a campfire—even with damp wood."

He pointed to the sheath. "See this stuff covering the blade? It's magnesium. You peel off a few slivers and dump them on a pile of sticks. Put a match to them, and the strips really flare up—instant campfire."

That annoying grin came back to his face. "Maybe, somehow, somewhere, Trouble Boy is going to get himself a high-tech hotfoot. I bet he won't know what to do."

Joe shook his head as Kevin swaggered off. It was obvious that Wylie was new to the prank business. Otherwise, he wouldn't be shooting his mouth off in front of witnesses. Did Kev really expect that no one would pass along a warning to Tom Gilliam? These kids were here to see a nice, exciting fight. If they had to, they'd push the two boys into each other. Kev seemed to think they were there to act as cheerleaders for him.

The doors opened, and the crowd poured in. Thoughts of a possible fight disappeared. Now people had to worry about forgotten homework and the possibility of pop quizzes.

As he headed for his homeroom, Joe debated warning Tom Gilliam himself. That magnesium could be dangerous stuff. It might cause more damage than Kev expected.

Then Joe shook his head. Was Kev Wylie really the type to give someone a high-tech hotfoot? Joe noticed that before Kev had said, "somehow, somewhere," he'd said "maybe."

No, Joe told himself, stepping up his pace to beat the first buzzer, Kev Wylie is all talk with very little action. No need getting Tom Gilliam stirred up. Joe paused at his homeroom door. And no need to get the new kid in any more trouble than he'd already made for himself.

When lunchtime came, Joe didn't join the mad dash for the cafeteria. He had decided he was sick and tired of the Kev and Tom show. Let the other idiots gawk at the latest episode.

Jingling the change in his pocket, he turned away from the crowd. Down this corridor, just before one of the less-used stairways, was a pay phone.

The day before, Joe's dad had spent some time reaching out to friends and colleagues. Joe suspected Fenton's morning had been spent receiving calls in return. How had that new information changed the profile of Russell Gilliam? Joe decided to find out.

He slipped coins into the slot of the pay phone and dialed his home. His aunt Gertrude answered. When she heard Joe's voice, she was worried that he was in trouble. Finally, though, she passed him along to Fenton.

"What's up?" his father asked.

"Oh, I got to thinking about Frank's crazy theory," Joe said. "Then I wondered what else you'd gotten on Russ Gilliam."

Fenton laughed. "As far as I can find out, he's never been in trouble with the law—officially. But right before he left his job at Dynodyne, his house burned down."

"There's a string of tough breaks," Joe said. "He lost his job, his wife and family, and even his house."

"Actually, it went this way: his house, his job, then his family," Fenton put in. "I haven't been able to clear up what happened at Dynodyne. The records don't show whether he quit or was fired.

"The local police and fire department haven't been very helpful about what happened to the house. But the court papers are pretty clear on the family issue. Mrs. Gilliam got an uncontested divorce."

"If Gilliam didn't try to hold on to his family, and the wife got custody of Tom, what's Tom doing with his dad now?"

Fenton paused for a moment. "Mrs. Gilliam passed away about a year and a half ago."

Joe took a deep breath. No wonder Tom had swung when Biff started talking about his mother.

"Joe?" his father said. "Did I lose you?"

"No, Dad," he replied. "Anything else new?"

"Not about Russell Gilliam," Fenton said. "The technical people finally finished with the car that nearly turned me into a hit-and-run statistic."

"Did they find any clues? Anything that might point to whoever was driving that night?"

"None, zip, nada." Fenton's voice had a what-can-you-expect? tone. "The police technicians said the car was cleaned very carefully. The report said, 'With surgical care.' "

"Con let you look at the report?" Joe asked in surprise.

"He hoped it might stir something to help with the investigation." Fenton sighed. "Looks as though all they're doing is hitting dead ends."

Joe knew how that felt. "So, even though that driver acted like a maniac, he *was* a pro. Or at least the driver's boss was a pro and cleaned away any possible evidence." He hesitated for a second. "Did you mention Frank's little theory?"

"No point to it," his father said. "There are some odd things going on in Gilliam's life, I'll admit, but that doesn't make him a traveling racketeer. Right now I'm more interested in tracking that wild

69

driver—*and* the pearl necklace he got away with. As for Gilliam—well, no sense making trouble for him."

"So you're closing the file on Russ Gilliam?" Joe asked.

"Unless something startling comes up, yes."

"I guess I can see why," Joe said, but he had a strange, dissatisfied feeling.

"Catching your brother's hunch?" Fenton asked, chuckling.

Joe laughed. "Well, I'm usually the one who has them. Thanks, Dad. See you later."

He hung up and stepped away from the pay phone. As he did, he spotted Tom Gilliam going up the stairs.

Maybe it was the way Tom was moving that made Joe follow him. The red-haired teen climbed the stairway cautiously, as if he were someplace he shouldn't be.

Strictly speaking, that was true. Tom was supposed to be in the cafeteria. For that matter, so was Joe.

A plastic soda bottle dangled from the fingers of Tom's right hand. That was another infraction of the rules: no eating or drinking in the halls and stairways.

Somehow, though, Joe suspected that was the least of what Tom was up to.

Fenton's words came back to Joe. "No sense

making trouble for someone." He still found himself following Tom.

Maybe I can stop some trouble before it happens, Joe told himself. He was a little slower going up the stairs, since he had to make sure Tom didn't hear him. So, when Joe reached the second floor, Tom was nowhere in sight.

A second later, though, Joe heard a distinctive metallic clang. It rang out from a corridor that branched off to his right. Joe knew that sound—he had heard it dozens of times a day. It was the sound of a locker door slamming closed.

Joe came around the corner to see Tom at the far end of the hall, moving pretty quickly.

One other thing Joe noticed was that Trouble Boy no longer had the soda bottle. Had he stashed it in his locker?

Oh, no. Joe's stomach sank as he remembered something he'd heard at the beginning of the school year. Kev Wylie had been complaining to Frank about the lousy locker he'd been assigned. It was in the least convenient corner of the second floor, Joe recalled.

Joe scanned both walls running along the corridor. Each wall was crammed with a double row of lockers. Which one was Kev's?

A bubbling noise brought Joe's attention to the right-hand wall. There—in the top row, about midway down the hall. A cloud of brownish smoke

71

began seeping out of the vents in one of the locker doors.

Joe headed in that direction, then quickly stepped back gagging. A smell like the mother of all sewers drove him away from the locker.

A stink bomb! Joe thought. Of all the stupid—

That was when something went wrong—terribly wrong.

A glare of light, like a photographer's flash multiplied by a hundred, burst from the vents in the metal door. Half-blinded, Joe stumbled back.

Even so, he could see the smoke and flames erupting through the openings in the locker door.

9 The Truth and Nothing But . . .

Joe spun around and ran back the way he'd come. Right before that last turn, he remembered he had passed a niche with a fire extinguisher. Yes! There it was!

He opened the case and pulled out the heavy canister.

A girl came down the stairs and spotted him. She froze halfway down the staircase, gaping at him.

"Get downstairs and sound the fire alarm," Joe said. "Somebody's locker has gone up."

Spotting wisps of smoke coming around the corner, the girl scampered away. Joe lugged the extinguisher toward Kev Wylie's locker. The hallway had pretty much disappeared in thick smoke.

It had a chemical tang that burned at Joe's lungs.

Coughing and choking, he made his way to the dull red glow of the fire. Joe jammed the extinguisher's cone-shaped nozzle against the vents in the locker door. He pulled the trigger, and foam spewed out of the extinguisher, filling the locker. The smoke began to thin as the burning books and whatever else was inside were smothered.

Joe could still feel the heat, though. The flash he'd seen—it had to be that magnesium fire-starter Kev had been showing off!

Joe knew that magnesium burned very hot and continued to burn even under water. Was there enough of the magnesium in there to cut through the bottom of the locker?

Joe didn't know. He just did his best to keep the blaze contained with the extinguisher in his hands.

Just as the canister ran out of foam, Mr. Sheldrake appeared with another extinguisher. He followed Joe's example, squirting the frothy white foam into the vents in the locker. The stuff was going in the bottom vent and overflowing out the top openings. Joe suddenly realized his shoes were soaked.

Then he heard shouted orders and heavy footfalls tramping up the stairs. The professional firefighters had arrived. Armed with even more extinguishers, the newcomers took up the battle.

A fire captain approached Joe and Mr. Sheldrake. In his gas mask and helmet, the man looked like something out of a bad science-fiction movie.

"Can you get that door open?" he asked.

"I have the master key—" Sheldrake began.

"There's something out of the ordinary in there," Joe warned. "I think it's magnesium."

Both men stared at him.

"Magnesium?" Mr. Sheldrake said.

"There was a big flash, and something in there is still burning," Joe said.

As the firefighters adjusted their game plan, Mr. Sheldrake led Joe back around the corner. Moments later the fire captain joined them. "All clear," he said. "The kid was right. There was a small piece of magnesium in the locker. Looks like it came from one of those survival firestarters campers use."

"Firestarter?" Mr. Sheldrake repeated. "You mean this was set deliberately?"

The fire captain shot a glance at Joe. Then he took the assistant principal aside. After a few moments' agitated discussion, Mr. Sheldrake was back.

"Did you see anyone fooling with that locker?"

"No." Joe was able to answer truthfully.

He *hadn't* seen Tom at Kev's locker. Tom was already at the far end of the hallway when Joe arrived on the scene.

Joe wasn't sure why, but he didn't want to rat on Tom Gilliam. Yes, Trouble Boy had planted a smoke bomb. But the disaster had been caused by the high-tech hotfoot gizmo Kev had in the locker.

This was a serious situation. Tom didn't face a slap-on-the-wrist lecture, detention, or even a suspension. An accusation of arson could get him bounced out of school. He could wind up in Juvie Hall, or even be charged as an adult and do real jail time. It all depended on how harsh the school board wanted to be.

The members of the board would probably take their cue from Mr. Sheldrake. And the assistant principal had plenty of reason to throw the book at Tom Gilliam.

Mr. Sheldrake knew how to question kids. He knew when he wasn't getting the whole story. The assistant principal did his best to loom over Joe. "And what were you doing up here?" he demanded suspiciously. "Where were you supposed to be? In class? In the cafeteria?"

"I decided to avoid the first rush to lunch," Joe replied. "There was something I needed to discuss with my dad. So I called him from the pay phone downstairs—"

"And what brought you up here?" Old Beady Eyes was really pushing it.

Joe had known the question was coming. And he knew a direct answer would sink Tom.

"There was a funny smell," he said, fast-forwarding his story. "I went to check, and there was smoke coming out of the locker. Then came the flash I mentioned earlier. Next thing I knew, there was a fire."

"Do you know whose locker that is?" Sheldrake wanted to know.

Joe shrugged. Old Beady Eyes had asked what he *knew*, not what he suspected. "No."

The assistant principal pulled a cell phone out of his jacket pocket. He dialed and a moment later was speaking with the secretary in the general office.

"Mrs. Effingham," he said, "no need to be alarmed. The fire is out. Yes, it was in a locker—I want to find out whose. Locker two forty-seven."

Sheldrake waited for a moment, listened, then said, "Kevin Wylie. I see."

He turned to Joe again. "Did you see Tom Gilliam at that locker?"

"No." Joe again was able to answer in strict honesty.

"Did you see him *near* the locker? Was he on the second floor?" Old Beady Eyes was really boring in with his cross-examination.

Joe did his best to look confused. "I don't know," he said. "There was someone at the far end of the hall—"

"A tall, skinny kid with red hair is pretty hard to

miss," Mr. Sheldrake cut him off. He hit Joe with his beadiest stare. "I know some students might hesitate at getting a classmate in trouble. That's false loyalty, Mr. Hardy. Your responsibility is to the whole school. Imagine what might have happened if you hadn't come along. This is very serious. You'll have almost three hours to think about it—before you see me after your last class."

Old Beady Eyes turned away. Joe was definitely dismissed for the time being.

His shoes still squishing from flame-retardant foam, Joe headed for his next class.

The end of the school day came all too quickly. Reluctantly, Joe set off for Mr. Sheldrake's domain. Joe had already told Frank he'd be late getting home. He hadn't discussed why—no sense getting big brother sucked into this mess.

Eyes fixed gloomily on his still-damp shoes, Joe headed for the Executioner's Block. That was the joking name for the bench outside the assistant principal's office. The name didn't exactly seem funny right then.

Joe had almost reached the bench when he stopped short. A pair of long legs ending in scuffed running shoes blocked his way. The Executioner's Block was occupied.

Joe raised his eyes to see Tom Gilliam. Trouble Boy gave him a wry smile, but his eyes were uneasy. Had he spotted Joe behind him during his little prank? More likely, the school grapevine had been at work. Tom knew Joe had been on the scene. What he didn't know was what the younger Hardy had actually seen.

The office door swung open, and there was Mr. Sheldrake. "Ah, gentlemen, right on time." He pointed to Tom. "I think I'll talk to you first."

Tom rose, and Joe dropped onto the bench, resting his head against the tiled wall.

The assistant principal's office had a door with a large frosted-glass window. From where Joe was sitting, he could hear everything going on inside.

"I had quite an interesting time with Captain Menzies of the fire department," Mr. Sheldrake began. "He examined everything that was left inside a certain burned-out locker.

"It seems some student created a stink bomb using materials pilfered from the chemistry lab. Clever enough—if our young genius had used a glass bottle to carry it. Instead, a plastic bottle was used. Besides causing a foul smell, the chemicals managed to melt their container. Then this mixture reacted with some magnesium inside the locker. The result was a surprisingly effective firebomb."

Mr. Sheldrake paused for a second, but for once Tom Gilliam had nothing to say.

79

"Only dumb luck saved us from a blaze that could have gutted the whole school," the assistant principal went on. "Not to mention what it would have done to all the students. You might want to think of that."

"Yeah?" Tom's bravado might have been more convincing if he didn't have to clear his throat to go on. "Why is that?"

"Mr. Gilliam, let's not play games. You and Kevin Wylie had words several times in public. People were expecting a fight. You apparently backed down—possibly because your father works for Kevin's father. Then comes this botched prank—"

"If Wylie had something dangerous in his locker, he should be in trouble," Tom interrupted.

"He and his father will be seeing me this evening," Mr. Sheldrake said. "Right now, I'm talking to you. I know you're not stupid, Tom. I've seen your school records. You were doing quite well until you hit the road with your father. Straight A's in California. You were working well above grade level."

Sheldrake's voice hardened. "Maybe that allowed you to coast in the other schools you attended. But the curve has caught up with you now. Your work has fallen below average . . ." Old Beady Eyes paused for a second. "Especially in chemistry."

The assistant principal sighed. "What are we supposed to do with you?"

"Do?" Tom repeated. His voice had a nervous edge.

"Schools are supposed to do things for young people," Sheldrake said flatly. "Keep them off the streets. Educate them. Make them good citizens. Fix them, if necessary."

He paused. "For instance, if one of them tries to burn the school down."

"But I didn't—there wasn't—" Tom's voice suddenly got cold. "You have no proof of that."

"Just suspicion," Sheldrake agreed. "And concern. We may find ourselves in a situation where we have no choice. Where we have to call in the police . . . and Social Services."

"Why them?" That was definite worry coming from Tom.

"You seemed to be a normal, good kid while you lived with your late mother," Sheldrake said gently. "After a year and a half with your father, well . . . look where you are. As I said before, we're expected to do something."

"Something like foster care." Tom made the words sound like a curse. "Throw me into the system. You say I'm not stupid. I did a little research. How many families do you think keep teenagers. Especially—what's that nice word— 'troubled' ones?"

"I can't quote statistics." Sheldrake's voice was uneasy. This wasn't going the way he'd planned.

"No, you'll just turn me into one," Tom said bitterly. "Excuse me if I don't help you."

"Then excuse me," the assistant principal said coldly. "But I have to help *you*."

A moment later Tom was coming out the door, headed for detention. "You might consider your options," Mr. Sheldrake said.

"Yeah," Tom said. "All my options."

The assistant principal was not in a good mood as he began interrogating Joe. "Apparently, you have a very sensitive nose, Mr. Hardy. Sally Hynde took the same staircase you were on. She didn't smell anything."

"She was upstairs, I was down," Joe replied. "Who can say how the smoke—and smell—traveled."

Old Beady Eyes did his best, but he didn't get what he wanted from Joe. "I can't say I saw anyone," Joe insisted. "I was trying to find where the smell came from. Then I saw the smoke. That's what I was looking at."

"Tom Gilliam had to be around there," Sheldrake insisted. "And you had to see him." He marched Joe to the detention hall next door. "Perhaps your time in here will help sharpen your memory."

Joe spent his silent hour about four feet from

Tom Gilliam. Every once in a while, Tom would turn his way. When Joe returned the glance, he saw the oddest look in the other boy's eyes.

At last Sheldrake appeared in the doorway, forced to let them go. He gave both boys his sourest look. "This is not over," he warned. "The investigation is just starting. You could do yourselves some good. Or you could do some irreparable harm to your permanent records."

Joe was just glad to escape. He walked quickly away from school when he realized he had a shadow. Tom Gilliam's long legs brought him up beside Joe.

"All right," the redheaded boy demanded. "Why didn't you give me up?"

"I didn't think it was fair," Joe replied. "With your rep, you'd have been out of school and maybe in jail. But Kev Wylie was equally stupid, bringing that magnesium fire-starter to school, and he'd probably end up only getting a stern lecture."

Joe glanced over at the other boy. "I heard some of your session with Old Beady Eyes. So I know you're not stupid. I'm cutting you a major break, here. Don't do something to ruin your life."

"My life hasn't been right for the last two years," Tom Gilliam said. "That's when my mom first got sick. I'll say this for my dad. Even though my parents were divorced when I was five, he sent money to my mom for doctors."

Tom shrugged. "Not that it did any good. When Mom died, the life we'd built in California died with her. I wound up living like a gypsy with Dad. Five towns in the last year and a half. Four different schools."

"Didn't you have any other relatives you could stay with?" Joe asked.

"Both Mom and Dad were only children," Tom said. "My grandparents have passed away, except for my dad's mother—she's in a nursing home." He shook his head. "My only choices are my dad . . . or foster care. They try to make the system work, but—"

"But what?" Joe asked.

"When I realized Mom wasn't going to be around much longer, I did some research. Too many kids just get shuttled from home to home. Kids my age can end up little better than slaves. You'd be amazed at how many people take in teenagers to get free labor."

Tom's expression was bleak. "Living like that, I might as well be in prison."

"Then you'd better make the best of living with your dad," Joe said.

"I know!" Tom angrily agreed. "But you don't know—" He stopped. "And I can't explain."

Joe decided to take a chance. He might get a punch in the mouth from the impulsive kid beside him. Then again, he might get some truth. "I know your dad is doing more than just the books at Tri-State Express," he said. "What's really going on there?"

Tom Gilliam looked at him for a long moment. "Since I came here, you're the first person who's been straight with me."

He took a deep breath. "So I'll tell you."

10 Whistle-blow-up!

Joe couldn't believe his luck in getting Tom Gilliam to talk.

As the other boy started, however, Joe couldn't believe what he was hearing.

"You saw how my dad lost it last Saturday when I made fun of whistle-blowers?" Tom said. "That's because he *is* one!"

"What?" Joe stared.

"Our whole life would have been different, Mom told me," Tom went on. "Dad was working for this high-tech company in Illinois. We had a nice home—that much I remember. Anyway, Dad was working on some defense contract. He found out his company was cheating the government."

"And he blew the whistle?"

"First, he tried to talk to his bosses. They just told him to keep quiet. But he didn't. Finally, he went to the government." Tom gave Joe a lopsided smile. "Even then he had a hard time getting people to listen to him. But in the end, Dynodyne was socked with a big fine. They paid it—and closed the plant where my dad had worked."

"And?" Joe asked.

Tom shrugged. "A lot of people in town lost their jobs, and a rumor went around that my father was responsible. Kids weren't allowed to play with me anymore. And then, one day, our house burned down."

Joe stared again. "Was the fire deliberately set?"

Tom spread his hands. "Who knows? The cops and fire department weren't much help. But then, they all had relatives who'd just lost what were supposed to be lifetime jobs."

"Sounds like a good incentive to leave town," Joe finally said.

Tom nodded. "No way Dad was getting a job around there. The fact was, he had a hard time getting a job anywhere."

"Is that why your folks split up?"

Hands in his pockets, Tom slouched along. "I guess it didn't help. Mom always blamed Dad for 'ruining things.' That's the way she put it. He wrecked his career and got us thrown out of town. And for what? Dynodyne is still around. They moved a lot of work down to Mexico."

Tom sighed. "And they're probably still cheating the government. Everybody does. It's not as though my dad got any reward for what he did. He wound up out a lot of money."

"So what happened?" Joe asked.

"As you said, Mom and Dad split up. Mom got me and all their savings. Dad—well, Dad just hit the road, working wherever he found a job. I thought he was just a glorified bum. But then he began sending us pretty big checks."

Joe stared yet again. I can't believe it! he thought. Is Frank going to turn out to be right?

"Where did the money come from?" he asked.

"It almost sounds funny," Tom said, shaking his head. "Dad made a career for himself as a whistle-blower."

"What?"

"He's become a professional whistle-blower," Tom explained. "He switches jobs often because he's always looking for companies with dirty little secrets."

"You're kidding me!" Joe burst out. "Wouldn't your dad get—well, a reputation?"

"If a company is clean, Dad just leaves. No reason to suspect why he was there. If not, there's a confidentiality clause in the agreement Dad makes with the bosses. They have to shell out even more if they reveal what Dad does."

Joe remembered Frank mentioning the generous payments Russell Gilliam got for leaving punky little jobs. This explained a lot. "So these companies buy your father off?"

Tom nodded. "They're supposed to clean up whatever wrongdoing he discovered. But how can you really check up on that?"

Another memory popped into Joe's head—a depressed Frank working at his computer. What had Frank said about whistle-blowers? "After all their sacrifices, they still end up not making a difference."

Maybe so, but it looked as though Russ Gilliam had discovered a way to make a living. "I guess your dad doesn't have to worry about job references. But why would a company hire a guy with three other jobs in the same year?"

"That's the beauty of his scheme. The fact that he doesn't look like a really steady type helps *get* him jobs. Companies pulling scams prefer workers who are just passing through." Tom laughed. "They're less likely to dig too deeply into a crooked operation."

Tom eagerly went on. "Sometimes, stockholders bring Dad in to check their companies out. That's sort of like what your dad does as a private eye. But—"

A worried frown appeared on Tom's face. "I think Dad's been doing this too long. He doesn't talk about making things right anymore. It's all about the payoffs." Tom slouched even more, jamming his hands in his pockets. He spoke so softly, Joe could hardly hear. "Where do you draw the line between being an idealist and being an extortionist?"

"I honestly don't know," Joe admitted, feeling the other boy's concern. "Do you think it might help to talk things over with my dad?"

"Maybe . . ." Tom said slowly. Then he grinned. "It would have to beat having a little chat with Mr. Sheldrake!"

The boys headed over to Oak Street and the Hardy home. Joe opened the front door. "Dad?" he called.

"Not in," Callie Shaw said, popping out of the living room. "He took your mom and Aunt Gertrude—oh."

She'd just spotted Tom Gilliam. Tom bristled in response.

"Joe? I invited the group—" Frank Hardy also seemed to run out of words when he spotted Tom.

Liz Webling appeared, her hands full of printouts. Then came Phil with some photos. Last of all came Kev Wylie.

His face went stiff when he saw Joe's companion. "Late as usual, huh, Gilliam?"

"Yeah," Tom shot back. "I had some burning issues to discuss back in school."

"So I heard," Kev snarled. "I guess a trial for arson is much more important than our dippy little project."

"Knock it off!" Joe demanded. "Nobody's going to trial. And who brought the hazardous metal and left it in his locker?"

"I—" Kev's mouth hung open until he closed it with a snap. "I guess Dad and I will have to talk about that with Mr. Sheldrake."

He swung round toward Tom again. "But that doesn't mean I have to—"

"Why don't you shut up and listen for a minute?" Tom demanded. "I came here to ask Mr. Hardy for some advice. But since you're here, I'll just go ahead and do what I was thinking about."

He took a deep breath. "The reason I know about whistle-blowers is because my dad is one. And, Kev, I think he's trying to get something on your dad's company."

Kev Wylie opened and closed his mouth several times, but nothing came out. To Joe, the guy looked like a fish. Then words came out in a sputtering rush. "I can't—You don't—what kind of a lousy—"

Kev was so indignant, he wasn't making any sense.

"Calm down," Frank advised. He looked at Joe.

"Can you explain this? Hopefully without insulting anyone?"

"It seems Tom's father is a professional whistle-blower," Joe said. "He found some hanky-panky going on in a company he worked for—Dyno-dyne."

He knew Frank would recognize the name. No need to advertise that the Hardys had been looking into Russ Gilliam's past.

"It was a bad experience," Joe went on. "But Mr. Gilliam figured out a way to turn it into a profitable business. He works for a while at various companies, checking whether they're on the up-and-up."

"That's the only way my father would run a company!" Kev Wylie burst out. "Who does your father think he is?"

"He thinks he's on the trail of something at Tri-State Express," Tom said. "I figure there's been enough trouble between us. This is my way of trying to clear things up."

"Do you know what your dad is on the trail of?" Liz Webling was every inch the junior reporter as she asked the question.

"No," Tom admitted.

"And even if he did, it would be off the record," Joe quickly put in.

"I guess you've had a rougher time than we imagined." Phil gave Tom a shrewd glance. "You

92

weren't just hitting a new town and a new school. This must be like a never-ending undercover assignment."

Tom turned gratefully to Phil. "I'm tired of secrets," he said.

Callie stared as if she'd been punched in the jaw. Her whole view of Tom was being turned on its head.

Kev, however, was stubborn. "I don't know if I buy what you're saying," he said. "But I've got to talk to my dad—now!"

Tossing the notes in his hand on an end table, he headed right out the door. The other teens looked at one another. "Maybe we ought to leave, too," Phil said. In moments he, Liz, and Callie were at the door.

Tom followed them, glancing back in the doorway. "Thanks, Joe," he said. "For everything."

Joe was surprised. Tom's face, usually a tight, angry mask, seemed relaxed. For the first time since Joe had seen him, Trouble Boy seemed at peace.

Mr. and Mrs. Hardy and Aunt Gertrude arrived about half an hour later. Each carried a sack of groceries. "There are more in the car," Fenton said.

The boys helped unload, waiting to get their father alone so they could share this new twist in events. Fenton was concerned about the fire. But Joe was more interested in the way his dad reacted to Tom Gilliam's strange revelation.

"A professional whistle-blower?" Fenton said slowly. "More like an unlicensed investigator, I'd say."

When they got to Tom's bombshell warning to Kev, Fenton went almost poker-faced. His eyes got a faraway look for a moment. Then Fenton stared at Joe. "Could Tom have been making any of this up—maybe stretching the truth to impress you?"

"He sounded rock-solid, Dad," Joe answered.

Fenton gave a careful shrug. "Well, there's the end of your theory, Frank."

As he watched his father walk away, Joe suddenly felt like Mr. Sheldrake. Mr. Hardy definitely knew more than he was letting on.

Should I call him on it? Joe wondered. Maybe I'll get Frank's take first. I'll talk to him after dinner.

When Joe went up to Frank's room, he found his brother at work at his computer.

"More research?" Joe asked.

Frank grinned, keeping his eyes on the screen. "Nope. A hack attack. Let's see if I can find why Dad brushed off your story so quickly."

Every once in a while, Frank would test the security on Fenton's office computer. But, Joe thought, he'd never had an incentive to break in.

Joe came round to look over Frank's shoulder. He couldn't make any sense out of what was on the screen, but Frank could. He squinted, frowned, fired off commands from the keyboard. A string of figures ran across the monitor.

"Bingo!" Frank muttered. "We've got a window of opportunity."

Directory lists appeared, whizzing past at almost a blur.

"How can you read—" Joe began, only to be shushed.

"We could be thrown out at any second." Frank spoke through clenched teeth. "Let's see how far back—uh-oh!"

He hit a couple of keys, and the screen abruptly went blank. "Busted," Frank announced.

But after he hit a couple more keys, a document appeared on the screen. "Dad tries to keep up with the best antisnooping software possible. But this time I actually managed to snatch a file. I was trying to see how far back in his records I could get—"

He stopped talking at Joe's gasp and joined in reading. The file was dated about four months earlier. "Consultation with Hal Owens," read the title.

Hal Owens was Kev Wylie's grandfather, a well-off businessman with several companies.

As Joe read through the notes, he learned of a deal Owens had done. He'd turned over a failing company—Owens Rapid Delivery—to his son-in-law. Don Wylie had been pestering Owens for a more responsible job. Owens thought Wylie would learn a good lesson—being responsible for a business crashing.

The younger man had been whining to get more money. Owens had refused. He knew no bank would fund Wylie's fantasies of expanding the business. Yet the business had expanded. Money had poured in.

A nice success story? Owens thought not. He had hired Fenton Hardy to investigate his son-in-law and the business. This company should have failed months ago.

So how was Don Wylie suddenly—and suspiciously—making money hand over fist?

11 Hits . . .

Frank finished reading the file he'd hacked from his dad's computer. His lips pursed in a silent whistle. Then he looked at Joe.

"I was trying to see how deep I could get into Dad's archives," he said. "This was the oldest file I could reach."

"Some file," Joe said. "I knew Dad was acting funny when we told him about Mr. Gilliam. Now I understand that crack about unlicensed investigators." He ran a hand through his short blond hair. "What do we do now?"

"First, we let Dad know his computer is vulnerable," Frank said. "At least to a snatch-and-grab job."

He tapped on his keyboard, closing down the

computer. "Then we ask about Mr. Owens, Mr. Wylie, and Tri-State Express."

Fenton wasn't happy to learn that Frank had cracked his computer's security. He was even more unhappy when he heard what the boys had read in there.

"That's supposed to be confidential," he complained.

"Dad, this wasn't something we were looking for," Frank said.

Joe nodded. "It just fell in our laps. But now that it's here . . ."

Fenton made a sour face. "Those notes are all there is to it. The case was pretty open-and-shut. Owens had an ambitious son-in-law. But Hal didn't think Don Wylie had the ability to match that ambition. Owens set Don up to fail."

"Nice guy," Joe said.

Fenton shrugged. "Business people sometimes pull stunts like that. It could be a trap to crush a rival. Sometimes it can teach an associate important lessons."

"Like that old saying," Frank said. " 'What doesn't kill me makes me stronger.' "

"Something like that," Fenton said.

"The problem is, Don Wylie didn't learn his lesson," Joe said. "He made the company profitable—very profitable."

"That's what brought Owens to me," Fenton

said. "He'd been cutting back expenses at the company to hold his losses down. Wylie wanted to spend money, to expand."

"Looks like Wylie was right," Frank said.

"Owens didn't think that way." Fenton frowned. "He wouldn't invest in his own company, and he made sure no banks would lend any funds. So, when Wylie began spending money anyway, he was convinced something crooked was going on."

"A *really* nice guy," Joe said.

Fenton nodded. "What's why I didn't agree to investigate. It sounded like a case of sour grapes to me."

He leaned back in his office chair. "When you told me about the 'service' Russ Gilliam offers—"

A light went on in Frank's head. "How he sometimes gets hired by suspicious stockholders," he said.

"Even if he is an 'unlicensed investigator.' " Joe grinned. "I'm only surprised you didn't react when Tri-State Express came up earlier in this case."

"It *didn't* come up in any case," Fenton quickly corrected him. "It was the place of work for someone whose background I was checking."

The boys' father frowned. "Although now, I have to admit—" He gave a little head-shake. "Maybe I should have nosed around a little more when Owens came to me."

❖ ❖ ❖

The next day at school Frank walked to social studies with Callie Shaw. "Nobody said Tom Gilliam had lost his mother!" She looked upset as they headed down the hallway.

"Everybody seems to be saying it now." Frank shook his head. The school grapevine must be working overtime. All of a sudden, Tom Gilliam had gone from "troublemaker" to "that poor kid."

"I was really mean to him." Callie's words came out almost as a groan. "How am I going to face him in class anymore?"

"Maybe you'll be able to do him a favor," Frank suggested, grinning. "Shoot a couple of spitballs at him if he dozes off during Bannerman's lecture."

Callie gave him a look but said nothing as they went in the classroom door.

As usual, Tom Gilliam was the last in the room. But Callie shouldn't have worried about having to face him. Tom had eyes only for Kev Wylie.

"Hey, Kev," he said, looming over the other boy's desk. "I've got a really good anti-whistle-blower story for you. There's this company that I'm assured is completely honest. But when the owner finds out there's a whistle-blower on the payroll, he fires him."

Tom's eyes were blazing. He glared down at Kev, who twisted in his seat but said nothing.

"What do you think, Kev? Do you think there's a prejudice against people who blow the whistle on dirty doings?" Tom's voice grew louder. He leaned in toward Wylie's face. "Or maybe your father has something to hide in his wonderful company. After all, he fired my dad just about as soon as you got home last night!"

Mr. Bannerman arrived, cutting off what was becoming a very nasty scene. Frank shuddered at the way things might go in the cafeteria. When the period ended, he leaned over to Callie. "Get a hold of Tom. Keep him busy for as long as you can. And whatever you do, don't let him get near Kev!"

"How am I going to do any of that?" Callie demanded.

"You'll think of something," Frank said, flying for the door. "If all else fails, tell him you're sorry."

Mr. Sheldrake had a firm rule about running in the halls. If Frank didn't break that regulation, he certainly bent it on his way to the cafeteria. He caught up with Joe while the younger Hardy was still coming down the stairs.

"Your pal Tom had some whistle-blower news today," Frank reported. "Don Wylie fired Russ Gilliam last night. Tom's pretty steamed."

Joe looked shocked. "Oh, I bet," he finally said. He gave Frank a sharp glance. "And why are you rushing to tell me?"

"You're the closest thing Tom has to a friend at Bayport High. Try to keep him from flying off the handle. Think of Old Beady Eyes. He won't like it if Tom makes lunch-hour fights a regular school activity."

The boys posted themselves at the cafeteria entrance. Frank spotted a grim-looking Kev Wylie going in. Toward the end of the crowd was Tom Gilliam. He was trying to ditch Callie, who resolutely hung on to him.

"Tom!" Joe pushed through the crowd to grab the boy's other arm. "I just heard what happened."

For a second Tom almost took a swing. He was wound up more tightly than Frank had ever seen him.

Then Gilliam recognized Joe. "Sorry," he said. "This has got me to the point where I'm not seeing straight. High-and-mighty Kev and his great dad!" He looked mad enough to spit. Then he deflated like a leaky balloon. "I thought speaking out would bring . . . peace. Mr. Wylie would bring Dad in, they'd talk, that would be the end of it."

His face tightened again. "Instead, Dad got a call telling him not to show up for work, or on any Tri-State property—ever. They treated him like a dog!"

Frank could see different emotions in Tom's eyes. He was ashamed for, and by, his father. He was guilty now for giving his dad away. But there was an odder vibe of nervousness that Frank caught. Tom was deeply worried about something.

"So what's your father going to do now that his cover's been blown?" Frank asked.

That background worry flared in Tom's eyes. "He's gone nuts! I thought he'd just get out of town. But he says he's going to stay. He's not leaving till he finishes with Tri-State Express!"

Frank and Joe spent the trip home from school in thoughtful silence.

"You think Mr. Gilliam was just shooting off his mouth about seeing the job through?" Joe finally asked. "With no job, I don't see how he can hope to dig up any dirt at Tri-State. And how's he going to pay his bills?"

"Tom said Mr. Gilliam makes big bucks from his business," Frank said. "Don't be fooled by the little apartment and the rusty car. I'll bet Mr. G. has lots of money to carry on a private war."

"That's what it is now—a war—isn't it?" Joe sighed. "Now I wish Tom had had a chance to talk to Dad before he did what he did. Tom hoped to straighten things out between himself and Kev. Instead, he's caused twice as much trouble."

"I guess trouble is Mr. Gilliam's business." Frank's gaze suddenly sharpened. "But I wonder if he's ever been busted in the middle of a case. He certainly doesn't have any back-up."

Joe slowly nodded. "Maybe we should keep an eye on him. How's the homework situation?"

Frank looked at his brother. "I took care of most of it during study hall."

"Me, too," Joe said. "We'll blast through the rest, get some supplies, and set up our own stakeout!"

A call to Tom was answered by Mr. Gilliam instead. He was rather curt with Frank, but Frank didn't mind. He just wanted to make sure the man was home. Joe parked the van across the street from the apartment house where the Gilliams lived. Then the boys settled in to watch—and wait.

"I don't mind missing supper," Joe said around a mouthful of sandwich. "But how late are we going to keep this up?"

"As late as we need to," Frank replied. "I'm betting we won't have to hang out for a midnight raid. Gilliam made his move pretty early the last time."

"Yeah, but that was a Saturday night, and I don't think it was planned. He had an argument with Tom and bombed out of there."

"Well, it's dark now," Frank said. "Let's give it a few more hours."

They were just about to give it up when Mr. Gilliam appeared in the doorway of the building. He moved more slowly than he had the night they had followed him. His car started up on the first try. Joe waited until the rusty tan sedan was around the corner before starting his own engine.

From there on, their surveillance was almost a

replay of their last trip. The only change came at the very end.

Gilliam pulled up about two blocks from the Tri-State warehouse and parked. Joe went past and turned the next corner. As he slowed down, Frank already had the door open. Out of the car and onto the sidewalk, he was watching Gilliam's car in seconds.

The tall, stoop-shouldered man was out of the sedan, walking up the block. Frank pulled back into the shadows as Gilliam passed.

Joe appeared at Frank's elbow. "Guess he's stashing his car here so it won't be recognized."

Frank nodded. "The question is, is he trying to get in—or is he meeting someone?"

They set off after Gilliam, sticking to the shadows. Both boys moved with a minimum of noise. A careless footfall could get them spotted.

Moving cautiously, they let Gilliam develop almost a block's lead on them. A second figure appeared from the shadows about half a block ahead. Joe looked ready to charge, but Frank held him back.

"That could be a contact, checking things out," he whispered.

Joe nodded in the darkness.

The strange, silent procession continued until Gilliam almost reached the brightly lit block that housed Tri-State's warehouse. Then the whistle-blower's new shadow made his move. Suddenly he had a short club in his right hand. He ran for Gilliam. So did the boys.

"Watch out!" Frank yelled.

Gilliam heard the cry. He raised an arm as his attacker charged in.

"Keep your nose out of where it ain't wanted!" grunted the shadowy attacker.

Backing up his words, he raised his arm and brought the short club down in a vicious swing—aiming for Gilliam's head!

12 ... And Misses

Joe raced ahead of his brother, getting to the men first. Russ Gilliam managed to block his attacker's first swing with his arm.

The move saved his skull, but he cried out in pain, and his arm fell useless at his side. The attacker wound up for another try.

By now Joe was on the scene. He threw himself at the attacker and landed on his back, trying to turn him around. But the attacker had a secret weapon.

Joe choked on a horrible odor. It was a weird mix—part expensive cologne, part unwashed flesh and clothes. Apparently Gilliam's assailant didn't believe in showers or deodorant. His body odor was enough to knock out an elephant. It actually had Joe's eyes watering.

The smelly attacker tried to swing his club back to get a crack at Joe. Frank arrived just in time to grab the guy's wrist.

Still struggling, they staggered back into a dim beam of light thrown from over a warehouse door. Frank's expression would have been funny if they weren't fighting a vicious and determined foe.

Frank's lips were tight, his nostrils pinched. He was trying to wrestle the club from the guy without breathing.

The attacker twisted free, bringing the club up again. His raised arm just made the stench worse. Joe suddenly wondered what might be living in the guy's clothes if he smelled this bad.

Joe snapped off a kick. He caught the guy in the thigh, staggering him. The club swept past Frank, a clear miss.

The man wore a hooded sweatshirt, the hood more like a cowl. It kept most of his face in darkness. Joe could just make out the whites of the guy's eyes. The man's gaze darted from one Hardy to the other.

Joe could follow his reasoning. The mystery attacker had lain in wait to put some major hurt on Russ Gilliam. The intervention of the Hardys added witnesses—and two more opponents. He had to size them up—to choose whether or not to attack.

The man swung his club, not in attack, but to keep the Hardys back. Then he suddenly whipped around and took off.

Frank made a halfhearted attempt to grab the guy because he had as many doubts about the man's hygiene as Joe did. Anyway, the guy darted into the blackness of a nearby alley mouth.

Joe took a step, then shook his head. Going up against someone with a club in pitch darkness wasn't a good game plan. He joined Frank, who'd run over to see how Russell Gilliam was doing.

Tom's father stared at them, his eyes huge in his pale face. The man's stoop was more exaggerated, and he cradled his right arm in his left hand.

"Is it broken?" Frank asked in concern.

"I-I'm not sure." Gilliam's voice was shaky as he looked from Frank to Joe. "Now I know where I saw you. That group of kids who came to the door—"

"Frank and Joe Hardy," Frank introduced themselves. "Our dad is Fenton Hardy, the private detective."

Gilliam turned to Joe. "Tom told me you tried to help him," he said. "You were taking him to see your father. Instead, he met Kevin Wylie."

Joe braced himself. He knew how this man could react when he was annoyed.

But Russ Gilliam only sighed. "I suppose Tom thought he was doing the right thing."

"I think your son is worried that you've stopped trying to shake things up," Joe said. "And started to shake companies down."

"Looks like he'd be right to worry tonight." Frank carefully took the man's arm. "And I'd say you were pretty shaken up."

Gilliam winced at the gently probing fingers. "Something is going on at Tri-State. Their accounting system is a joke. I kept stumbling across unexplained cash coming in."

"It's going to be hard, trying to follow the money from outside," Frank said.

"I got a call tonight," Gilliam went on. "One of my co-workers. Said word had gone around about why I'd been fired. He wanted to help. Suggested a meeting down here."

Gilliam sucked in his breath with a hiss as Frank tried to roll up his sleeve. "Obviously a trap."

"I don't know if it's much consolation," Joe said, "but I think this was meant to scare you more than anything else. You even got a warning, to keep your nose out of where it didn't belong."

He tried a joke. "I just wish I could have kept my nose away from the guy with the warning!"

Gilliam managed a wan smile. "He was pretty ripe, wasn't he?"

"Fonder of perfume than soap, that's for sure,"

Frank said. "I think we'd better get that arm to a hospital. I don't think it's broken. But then, I don't have X-ray vision."

There was no way Gilliam could drive his car. The brothers gave him a lift in the van.

Luckily, it was a quiet night for the emergency room of Bayport General. The good news was that Russell Gilliam had a nasty bruise instead of a broken arm. He still got to wear a sling as a souvenir of his encounter with the smelly thug.

"Thanks for your help," Gilliam said. "Both now—and before."

"Are you going to stay on this?" Joe asked.

"I've gotten threats before," Gilliam responded.

Frank frowned. "Were they usually backed up with a medium-size stick?"

"Son, I had my house burned down. As you said, it was a warning." Gilliam had a stubborn look on his face. "Don Wylie can throw me off his company's property, but he can't get me out of town. I intend to keep an eye on him—maybe I'll find out where the mystery money comes from."

The whistle-blower adjusted his arm in the sling. "At the very least, my presence will help shake Wylie up. Whatever he's doing, he's no criminal genius. Sooner or later, he'll make a mistake."

"Like maybe hiring El Stinko to attack you?" Joe asked.

"Mistakes like that can be dangerous for you, too," Frank said.

"I wasn't expecting it," Gilliam said defensively. "I'll be on my guard now."

He insisted on taking a taxi home. Joe and Frank drove off to Oak Street in worried silence.

"I begin to see Dad's point about unlicensed investigators," Joe finally said. "Gilliam may be great at following the numbers—"

"But he's not used to the rough-and-tumble side," Frank finished. "Somebody's taking this pretty far for a business scam."

"You don't think it's Don Wylie?" Joe asked.

"Could you see Kev hiring someone for a stunt like that?" Frank shot back. "Of course, I don't know his father very well. But the picture I get from Kev—and even from Mr. Owens—is of a would-be executive."

"Someone who'd send a lawyer instead of a thug," Joe said. "So who set Gilliam up? Who sicced the Smelly Menace on him?"

Sitting in the passenger seat, Frank only shook his head. "I have no idea." He held up a finger. "No, I have one. Let's talk to Dad."

Fenton was watching the television news when the boys got in. "You're in late for a school night," he said. "What's going on?"

Joe and Frank gave him their own news report. Fenton leaned forward when he heard about the attack on Russ Gilliam. But he got really interested when they started to describe the attacker.

"A slim man, young enough and agile, if he broke free," Fenton summed up. "You couldn't get a good look at his face because of the hood. But—" He tapped his nose. "You got a good whiff of cologne and rancid flesh."

Frank nodded. "Guy smelled as if he hadn't had a bath in a month of Saturdays." He frowned. "But the stink-water was expensive. One of those designer jobs—you know, fifty bucks an ounce."

Fenton almost jumped from his seat. "Bad body odor covered by expensive perfume. You know who that describes? Stinky Peterson!"

Joe stared. "The burglar who handed over the pearls to that guy in the car?"

"I wondered how he got that silly nickname," Frank said.

Fenton smiled. "In this case, his nickname is purely descriptive."

Joe wasn't paying much attention. He squinted his eyes, trying to remember what the man in the rain had looked like. Then Joe shook his head. It had been too dark, too murky. He couldn't match up any features with their attacker that night.

"Why would a burglar attack a whistle-blower?" Frank wanted to know.

"I can think of one reason," Fenton said. "Because he had to. Because his fence told him to."

"This would be the same guy who burned down the rival pawnshop?" Frank asked.

"For a specialized job, they probably brought someone in," Fenton replied. "But as the new boys in town, they'd be spread pretty thin."

"Short of muscle," Joe said thoughtfully.

"So they asked Stinky to put a scare into Gilliam," Fenton finished. "He's on the lam right now. A little help—or money—would come in handy."

Frank nodded slowly. "I was saying to Joe that I couldn't see Don Wylie hiring a leg-breaker to intimidate someone."

"Threatening legal action would be more his style," Joe said. "Just like Kev. Lots of talk, not much done."

Frank frowned more deeply. "But why would the new fence in town be going after Mr. Gilliam?"

"I think it's time to go back to your theory," Fenton said. "Turned around a little. Gilliam isn't the front man for the mob. He's threatening to blow the whistle."

"On what?" Joe asked. He couldn't quite believe what he was hearing.

"On the connection between the new fence in town and Tri-State Express!" Frank's voice rose with excitement. "That's the source of the mystery money Wylie has been using to expand the business."

Joe nodded. "In return, this foreign gang gets a very respectable pipeline out of Bayport."

"More than that," Fenton put in. "By expanding, Tri-State puts offices and warehouses in other towns, other states—"

"Other places to set up fences and move goods!" Joe realized.

"Gilliam had part of the puzzle by looking at Tri-State's books," Fenton said.

Joe leaned eagerly forward. "And we had another—because you were tracking those pearls, Dad."

"Put it all together, and you get a pretty ambitious picture." Frank looked from his brother to his dad. "At least the start of something big."

"It's still only a theory," Fenton warned. "Although the facts we know hang together pretty well."

"Better than my original idea," Frank had to admit.

"I'll pass it along to Con Riley tomorrow," Fenton said. "We'll see what proof the local force can dig up to fill in the gaps."

He and Joe shared a cheerful smile. But Frank didn't join in.

"That's great," he said. "But we still have Mr. Gilliam out there, who thinks he's dealing with a local business scam."

"Okay, we'll pass our theory on to Tom tomorrow at school." Joe checked his watch. "And unless we want to be zombies in class, we'd better hit the hay pretty soon."

Joe kept an eager eye on the other students as he went into school. But he didn't spot Tom Gilliam anywhere in the thundering herd.

Isn't that the way things work out. When you don't want to see people, they're always underfoot. But the minute you need to find them . . ."

He did see Liz Webling coming out of her first-period class. Joe peered into the classroom. "You have math with Tom Gilliam, didn't you?" he asked.

Liz shook her head. "Not today," she said. "Maybe he's sick."

Kev Wylie came down the hall. "Sick of school," he sneered.

Liz followed the boy with her eyes. "I guess he's glad not to have Tom around."

"Yeah" was all Joe said as Liz set off for her next class.

Anybody could get sick in this place, he told himself as he hurried down the hallway. There are probably enough germs in the air to infect the whole town.

So why did he have such a bad feeling about what Liz had said?

Joe's next class was English. Today Ms. Browning was holding the class in the school library. As Joe came down to the first floor, he found himself walking past the dreaded Executioner's Block.

Suddenly he felt someone grab his arm. Joe turned to confront Russell Gilliam.

Tom's father still had his right arm in a sling. "They gave me pain medication in the hospital last night," he said. "I just woke up."

Gilliam looked awful. Something far worse was wrong with him than the pain in his arm.

"Are you all right?" Joe asked.

Russell Gilliam didn't seem to hear. "There was a message on my answering machine. It was from your Mr. Sheldrake. It was a truancy check. Tom hadn't shown up for school . . ."

The man's eyes finally focused on Joe. They burned with worry.

"He's supposed to be here, Joe. I—I don't know where Tom is!"

13 Desperate Moves

At the end of social studies, all Frank knew was that Tom Gilliam hadn't shown for class. Before Frank got to lunch, though, he'd heard three rumors "explaining" Tom's absence.

Joe stood waiting at the cafeteria entrance. Frank listened closely as his brother reported the scene with Russell Gilliam.

"He was demanding to see Mr. Sheldrake," Joe finished. "I don't know what Old Beady Eyes can tell him."

"Sheldrake probably believes Tom had second thoughts about that arson charge and skipped," Frank said grimly. "Even though that's a lot less colorful than the other stories I've been hearing."

"Which are?" Joe asked. "The one about Tom knocking over the convenience store? And being on the run from the cops?"

"There was one about flying saucers and alien abductions." Callie grinned, joining the conversation.

Her face fell as she took in the serious expressions on the boys' faces. "Not funny, huh?" she said. "You don't think something happened to Tom, do you?"

The brothers' silence shook her up.

"But Mr. Sheldrake is treating it as a case of truancy," she said.

"Of course, we know how highly Old Beady Eyes values Tom's presence," Joe responded.

"Come on, guys. We've learned that Tom had a pretty rough time, and we're sorry for him." Callie leaned forward. "But that doesn't mean he's an angel. Are you a hundred percent sure he didn't decide to skip school?"

She saw Phil Cohen in the crowd and beckoned him over. "Let's see what a neutral bystander has to say. Phil, what do you think about this Tom Gilliam thing?"

Phil shook his head. "I don't know what to think. Tom could be a real pain. But I don't remember him ever cutting classes before."

"Not you, too, Phil!" Callie burst out. "Frank and Joe are acting as if—" She broke off, noticing someone edging backward into their group.

Although her back was to him, Frank recognized Liz Webling. "Hey, Liz," he said. "Trying to get a scoop for the rumor mill?"

Liz turned around, only a little embarrassed that they'd caught her eavesdropping. "I was hoping to get a little truth. It might help balance all the nonsense people keep telling me."

She looked at Frank and Joe. "Some kids noticed Mr. Gilliam was wearing a sling. They're saying he and Tom went at it last night. Now Tom's heading out of town."

Joe exploded. "That's not true—I know how Mr. Gilliam got his arm wracked up last night—"

Frank shot his brother a warning glance.

"And—um—that wasn't it," Joe finished feebly.

Liz, Callie, and even Phil wanted to hear more. Frank cut them off. "Let's just say it had something to do with Mr. Gilliam's whistle-blowing activities. Can we leave it at that?"

His answer was definitely not enough for Liz. The would-be reporter leaned closer. "Do you think Tom's disappearance might tie in with whatever happened last night?"

"I don't know." Frank couldn't keep the worried tone from his voice. "I just don't know."

Frank and Joe headed straight home after school. That night was the charity auction, and their mom and aunt Gertrude would have left early to get everything prepared.

But Dad should be home, Frank thought. I really want to hear what he has to say about Tom dropping out of sight.

As the boys came down their street, however, they found an unexpected visitor. Russ Gilliam's rusty tan car was parked in the Hardy driveway.

The whistle-blower leaped up from the porch steps as the boys came into sight. "Do you know where your father is?" he asked sharply.

"We thought he'd be in the house," Frank answered. "Since I'm sure you rang the bell, looks like he's not here."

Gilliam's stooped shoulders sagged a little more. "You mentioned last night that he was a detective. I want to hire him."

"Because of Tom?" Frank asked.

Russell Gilliam nodded. "Your Mr. Sheldrake is convinced Tom was just cutting classes. The police have the same opinion." Gilliam's expression grew more sour. "Although there are some who suspect he may be a runaway."

Frank and Joe exchanged a glance.

"I spent the afternoon being shuffled from one office to another," Gilliam went on. "Never saw a police department so unwilling to take a missing persons report."

"Local law sets a period of seventy-two hours

before they start looking for an adult," Frank said.

"But I thought they started searching immediately for kids," Joe put in.

"Unfortunately," Mr. Gilliam said, "Tom's a teenager—he seems to fall into a crack in that law. I was told to wait to see if he turned up after school. Then I was sent home to check if any money or clothing was missing."

"That's the runaway theory," Joe said.

Russell Gilliam appeared to be numb. "Tom and I weren't always happy together. But no matter how tense things got, there was one thing he hated more."

"Foster care," Joe said.

The older man nodded. "He hated the whole idea, and he knew that's where he'd wind up if he took off."

"When did you last see Tom?" Frank asked.

"Last night, when I got home after our little adventure," Gilliam answered. "It was pretty late, but Tom was up, worried about me."

Gilliam shrugged, gesturing toward his sling with his good hand. "When Tom saw this, he was pretty upset. "He thought I should have brought him along as backup. Finally, we went to bed. The doctor in the emergency room had given me some pain pills. I took one, and it knocked me out until the phone woke me up. That was Sheldrake calling from the school."

"Was anything out of place?" Frank asked.

Gilliam shook his head—an emphatic no. "Tom's schoolbooks were gone. There were breakfast dishes drying by the sink." Tom's dad managed a wan smile. "He left just enough milk for me to have a cup of coffee."

The whistle-blower's face hardened. "It was the usual setup for a schoolday—except Tom never made it to school." Gilliam's faded gray eyes suddenly flashed. "And what happens? That fool Sheldrake starts yammering about Tom's permanent record. Meanwhile, the police want a recent photo so they can keep an eye on nearby bus depots."

He calmed down a little. "I did have an intelligent conversation with an officer named Riley. He had some pointed questions to ask about Tri-State Express."

Gilliam sighed. "He was honest enough to admit he couldn't help me unless"—the man's voice stuck—"unless there's evidence of a crime."

Frank hated seeing the pain on Gilliam's face. "Look," he said. "We'll do our best to pass on a message to our dad for you. But right now I think the place you ought to be is home. If there's any news—any . . . contact—that's where it will be coming in."

"You're right, son." Gilliam gave a tired nod. "That's where I'm heading. Tell your dad. You have my number? Here—just in case." He awkwardly scribbled the phone number with his left hand.

Silently, Frank and Joe watched as Russell Gilliam drove off. Inside the house, they found a note from Fenton.

> Boys—
> A friend on the New York City force has a lead on the Nugent pearls. They seem to have turned up in the Big Apple. I'm off to help him check it out. Be back sometime late tonight.
>
> Dad

Frank tapped a finger against the sheet of paper. "I guess Dad would think that was good news. Not exactly the same for us."

"No place to contact him," Joe said. "I guess Mr. Gilliam will just have to wait until Dad gets back."

Picking up another piece of paper and a pen, Frank began writing. "But *we* don't have to wait."

Joe looked at his brother suspiciously. "What are you up to?"

"I'm leaving a message for Dad about Tom and his father." Frank finished writing. "Russ Gilliam doesn't know what to do or where to turn. But I've got an idea. Maybe it will blow up in my face. Maybe we'll end up with another door slammed in our faces. But I think it's worth a try before Dad comes home."

He led the way to the van and got behind the wheel. In moments they were heading for the outskirts of Bayport.

Both boys could remember a time when there were farms just outside Bayport. But Bayport had grown as they grew, and developers had bought the farms and put in whole neighborhoods of homes.

Frank steered the van toward a very fancy development. The houses here were more like mini-mansions.

Kev Wylie's dad had bought a home out here to celebrate his success.

It was a big house, but not many lights were on.

"Could they be away?" Joe asked.

"Everyone tends to hang out in the back," Frank replied. "In the kitchen or the family room." He went up the stoop and rang the doorbell.

Kev Wylie answered. He stood in the doorway with a cardboard container of Chinese food in one hand and a fork in the other.

"Frank! Joe!" He looked at them in surprise. "What's up?"

"We need to talk to you and your dad," Frank said.

"Um—we're having dinner right now."

Frank glanced at the box in Kev's hand. "So I see."

Kev's face went bright red. "Yeah—well."

He held the door open and led the way inside.

Frank and Joe followed Kev into a wood-paneled foyer with a skylight overhead. To the left was a formal dining room. On the right was a parlor right off the cover of *Expensive Living Magazine*.

Odd, Frank thought looking at all the fancy furniture. None of those chairs looks as if it's been sat in.

The thick carpet under their feet gave way to tile floors. Frank noticed a scuff here and there as they went into the huge eat-in kitchen. Sitcom laughter burbled from a TV on the counter, and the air was full of delicious smells.

Frank saw why. The table was strewn with boxes, foil bags, and plastic jars. It was a regular take-out feast.

Donald Wylie hunched over a steaming food container. He was trying to lift a piece of broccoli to his lips with a pair of chopsticks. The morsel fell when he noticed he had company.

"Hello, fellas." Kev's father looked a little embarrassed as he glanced at the mess. "Mrs. Wylie is out tonight, so it was just us guys for dinner. I guess we didn't see the need to get any plates dirty."

He gestured toward the spread on the table. "Feel free to join us. There are ribs, and we haven't even opened the chicken and peanuts—"

"Thanks, but I don't think so," Frank said. "We just came from a visit with a very upset Russell Gilliam."

Don Wylie looked grim. "After the trouble that family has caused us, we want nothing to do with them."

"But I think you may have something to do with the trouble they're having now," Frank said. "Russell Gilliam was attacked last night near your warehouse. We managed to stop that. But now Tom has disappeared. In spite of what's being said, there's no evidence he ran away. And kidnapping, I'd remind you, is a federal offense."

Kev leaped to his father's side, a look of outrage on his face. "Are you guys crazy?" he demanded. "You come in here—"

He stopped as the box of food dropped from his father's trembling hand and spilled across the table. "It's not my fault!" Donald Wylie said. "I was just going to set Gilliam up. Lure him to a meeting, take some pictures—I figured my lawyers could tie him up." Donald Wylie shook his head. "But Nicolai said he'd take care of it. As for this boy disappearing, I didn't even know about that."

"Who's Nicolai?" Joe wanted to know.

"He's a man who came to me, offering big payments for special handling on shipments going out of town. He told me he had businesses in several other towns—even in other states, and wanted us to serve them. With the cash he advanced, I was able to expand. We set up new offices, warehouses."

Wylie used a napkin to mop his face. "There was lots of new business. I never connected Nicolai's shipments with big burglaries and robberies." He took a deep breath. "Not at first."

Don Wylie's eyes were on the Hardys. But Frank could see the expression on his son's face. Kev went pale as all his pride and trust in his father came crashing down. "Dad," he said in a choked voice.

Don Wylie turned. "It's not my fault!" he said again, louder. "I wanted to show your grandfather I was ready for the big leagues. He was only using me as a glorified office boy. But he rigged everything against me. Tri-State would fail if we didn't expand. I needed money—couldn't get it from the bank or your grandfather."

"But you could get it from Nicolai," Frank said.

"I didn't know where it came from," Wylie protested. "It was there when I needed it. And when I finally found out, it was too late. Then this Gilliam guy. When Kev told me what he did, I had to tell Nicolai. He said—"

Wylie's flood of confessions was cut off as a man came through the rear door. He had a lean, craggy, weather-beaten face—the sort of face that's lived a rough life. Two bigger men stepped to either side of him. They were silent, brutal—even rougher looking.

"No more saying anything now," the stranger said, his voice accented.

Donald Wylie froze with his mouth open, staring at the newcomer. For Kev, Joe, and Frank though, only one thing had their attention.

That was the pistol in the man's hand.

14 Silent Partner

Joe Hardy managed to drag his eyes from the pistol barrel to the gunman's face. "Let me guess," he said. "You must be Nicolai."

The man gave him an ironic bow. "Am very same." He flashed a smile at Joe. And in this case, it really was flashy. Half of the guy's teeth had been capped—in stainless steel!

Nicolai stepped over to Mr. Wylie, who was still seated at the table. The foreigner shook his head. "Donald, Donald," he said. His accent made the name come out more like "Dahwnalt."

"Is this good for business?" Nicolai demanded. "Telling secrets to anyone who comes to our house? I thought you stronger man than this, Donald."

Wylie fought to regain some of his old assurance. "When were you going to tell me about that boy, Nicolai?"

"I wasn't," Nicolai replied. "Sometimes is good thing to have silent partner." His lips curved. But his smile was as hard as his steel teeth. "Better you keep silent."

"It's kidnapping, Nicolai," Frank said.

"Call it, rather . . . problem-solving." Nicolai gave a quick order to his muscle men. Whatever the language was, the enforcers understood it. One dropped a heavy hand on Donald Wylie's shoulder, urging him up. Then they began herding everyone out the back way.

"Very trusting people, Americans." Nicolai smiled as he slipped the gun into his jacket pocket. "They think screen door will protect whole house."

Joe marched with his brother in a grimly silent parade around the house. Nicolai stopped by the van. "Who drives?" he asked.

Frank took out the keys.

"Good. You and your brother, Mr. Wylie . . . and Yuri."

A gun popped into the hand of one of the big enforcers. He gestured for them to get in.

"What about Kev?" Mr. Wylie asked in a tight voice.

"Young man rides with Dmitri and me," Nicolai

responded. "Little reminder not to play at being heroes, eh?"

The second goon took Kev by the arm and led him off to a high-priced sedan parked behind the van. Joe had to admit that the bad guys' car fit the neighborhood better than his van did.

"We meet at Donald's warehouse," Nicolai said. He took a step toward his car, then turned back. "Please try not to be late."

Usually that was just an everyday phrase. But hearing it from the hard-faced man with the synthetic smile . . .

Joe couldn't manage to stop a little shiver from running down his spine.

Frank got behind the wheel of the van. Joe, Mr. Wylie, and the goon called Yuri got in the back.

Yuri didn't bother hiding the gun once they were inside. He propped it on his knee, covering his prisoners. Otherwise, he simply sat there, silent, like a large, menacing statue.

From where Joe was seated he couldn't get a good look at the route Frank was taking. He also couldn't see Nicolai's car.

Frank seemed to be taking it very easily. The van certainly wasn't making the trip at top speed. After all, they were out on the edge of town. Getting down to the Harborside area would take a while.

Joe hated being effectively blind. If he'd been

up front with Frank, they might have been able to spot a chance. Maybe they could pull away from Nicolai's shadow.

Instead, Joe could only sit and hope he would be ready for any hint from Frank. Maybe he could find some advantage over Yuri.

Frank's slow progress could be a setup. Let Yuri get used to a steady speed, and he might settle back. Then, a good tromp on the gas, hit the brakes—

The guard might be thrown, his aim distracted. Joe would have a chance to jump him. He tried to will himself to look relaxed, but it was hopeless. Joe could feel every muscle tightening in his body. Sneakily, he put more and more weight on his feet. If there was even a ghost of a chance . . .

Joe glanced over at Mr. Wylie. The businessman sat slumped in his seat, his gray face locked on Joe's. Donald Wylie's eyes silently begged Joe not to do anything foolish. The hopelessness of the situation crushed down on Joe like a ton of rubble.

He'd been dreaming. No move, no matter how fancy or bold, could set them free. Kev was in that other car, a hostage.

And, perhaps in the Tri-State warehouse, another hostage—Tom Gilliam—awaited them.

Joe tried telling that to his muscles, but they

133

wouldn't listen. Nor would they loosen. By the time the van arrived downtown, he was seriously afraid of cramps.

Finally they came to a stop and Frank turned off the engine. Light was coming through the windshield. At least it was brighter than elsewhere in this neighborhood.

A heavy hand banged against the van door. A hoarse voice shouted something in a foreign language.

Yuri finally stirred. Still keeping the gun on the prisoners, he jerked a finger toward the door.

Joe rose stiffly and opened the door. A new goon stood outside, also with a gun in his hand. He was far enough away that Joe couldn't get at him. The guy's position also allowed him to cover Frank, who was getting out of the front door.

Joining his brother, Joe stood blinking in the glare of the floodlights around the building. It was lit up like a Hollywood set. Unfortunately, the streets were deserted. No one was around to see what was going on. No one, that is, except the foreign gang members shoving the prisoners toward the office entrance.

Joe looked around as he was prodded through the door. Where is old Pops the night watchman when you really need him? Joe thought.

A moment later he got his answer. The security guard lay on the office floor, unconscious. His cap

134

was gone, and Joe saw a big, swollen bruise on the side of the man's head.

But the guard wasn't the only person in the office. Tom Gilliam and his father, both a bit the worse for wear, stood against a bank of filing cabinets. They were guarded by yet another foreign goon, and a slightly built man with a fleshy face. One whiff and Joe knew him immediately—Stinky Peterson.

The burglar handled the gun he held as if it were some strange awkward object. "More people?" he said in dismay.

"More problems," Nicolai corrected him. "Now they are all in one place." He paused for a second. "Now I solve them."

"Nicolai," Donald Wylie spoke up. "There's no problem that can't be solved with a little talk. You need me—you need my company."

He must have been practicing this speech all the way down here, Joe thought. But he sounds like a cartoon of a businessman entering negotiations. Wylie just can't keep the fear out of his voice.

Nicolai was in no mood to negotiate. "You become more trouble to me than you are worth, Donald." He sounded like a man clearing away the checkers after the game is over.

"The police begin to sniff around you." The gang leader nodded toward the Hardys. "If two boys can get my secrets out of you, what happens when you face real pressure?"

"Nicolai." Wylie licked his lips in nervousness. "Please—"

"Oh yes," Nicolai cut him off. "Always the same. 'Nicolai, please. Nicolai, I never tell.' " He thrust a grim face into Wylie's sweating one. "You going to make promises for everyone here? Six people, if you count old guard? He'll conveniently forget knock on head?"

The gangster pointed at the Gilliams. "They'll leave town and never come back?"

Then he turned on Joe and Frank. "They'll shut up just to please you?"

Finally he stood in front of Kev. "And your son . . . Pardon me that I say this, but—" Nicolai looked over at Don Wylie. "He has a big mouth. And now—to me, he looks mad at you."

Kev wasn't saying anything. But pure anger radiated off his sullen, silent face.

Shaking his head, Nicolai went back to Don Wylie. "No, I don't think you can keep so many people quiet. So we must be like businessmen. Take decisive action. Shut all inconvenient mouths—permanently."

"You're going to kill *all* of them?" Stinky Peterson was sweating even more heavily. That didn't make him any sweeter to be around.

Nicolai didn't seem to notice the frightful

stench. He leaned in until he was nose to nose with the burglar. "You do business with us, you do what we say. If not, you're just in our way."

Peterson turned away, and Joe watched him take in the row of captives. This was what happened to people who got in Nicolai's way.

"I guess you're glad you brought in some of your own boys." Joe tried hard to ignore the tightness in his throat as he spoke. "The local talent hasn't been much help to you."

"Shut up, you!" Peterson turned so abruptly, droplets of sweat flew off his face. The burglar's nerve was stretched to the limit. He brought up his gun. But his hand was shaking so badly, there was an even chance he'd miss—even at this close range.

Nicolai grabbed Peterson's gun hand, carefully bringing it back down. "No shooting," he said. "No St. Valentine's Day like old-fashioned gangsters."

He gestured to his thugs. One began pulling file cabinets open. Another produced a square metal can and began pouring its contents over the files.

The raw, sharp smell of gasoline filled the room.

"Terrible fires will destroy all records of Tri-State Express," Nicolai announced. "How sad. All inconvenient witnesses will also die in blaze."

"Like that pawnshop owner when his store went up?" Joe couldn't help himself. He was angry, and words were all he had for weapons.

Nicolai looked at him for a long, hard moment. "I think you have big mouth, too," he finally said. "I wonder how you'll do when all you have to breathe is smoke."

"You can't hope that the police will buy this as an accident," Frank said.

"Your police don't believe pawnshop fire was accident, either," Nicolai retorted. "But American police need evidence."

He pointed to his steel false teeth. "Police back home knocked out the real ones—on suspicion. My business partners couldn't send packages back home—police were sure to search them. So we found truck drivers, train crews who would work with us. In old days, needed passport to go from one city to another."

Nicolai gave them another steel smile. "America is much easier country to do business. Police may suspect much, but it will all be just theories. Did Gilliam and son come to burn place down? Did they get trapped with Donald and his son?"

He glanced at the Hardys. "Did these boys Hardys come to warn of planned arson? Who can say?" Those steel teeth flashed again in a mirthless smile. "Who's alive to say?"

Nicolai shook his head. "The police may wonder many things, but they'll never know."

He gave another command in his slurred native tongue. The muscle men who weren't preparing the arson began tying up Joe, Frank, and the Wylies.

"N-Nicolai." Don Wylie stumbled over the name as his arms were yanked roughly behind him. "We're not back where you came from now." The businessman's hands were bound. Now the goon went to work on his ankles. "We're in America. There has to be a better way than this. Please, Nicolai. *Please!*"

"I have one American dollar for every time I hear 'Please, Nicolai!' I could retire. Be very wealthy man." The gang boss pulled a wadded handkerchief from his pocket. He stuffed it into Wylie's mouth where he lay on the floor. "Shut up, Donald. Back home, all traitors get is bullet in back of head."

The pair of enforcers trussed up Joe and Frank while their partners continued to move through the warehouse. Joe could hear the splashing of gasoline. The raw stench of it drowned out even Stinky Peterson's reek.

"Better punishment, I think, to leave informer alive. Let him think about his mistakes as flames come to take him."

The huge room outside echoed with the efforts of Nicolai's arsonists. It has to be full of boxes and packing material, Joe thought. That stuff will go up like the Fourth of July. Did Wylie splurge for a sprinkler system?

Joe glanced at the unconscious guard. Cheap security—I'll bet on cheap fire safety, too.

A shout from the warehouse told Joe that the job was done, even if he didn't understand the words.

"Goodbye, my friends." Nicolai turned as one of his goons handed him a heavy hammer. The gangster stepped to the office door that led to the street. One sudden swing, and the doorknob was gone.

"No getting out that way now. I don't think anyone will notice—not when fire is finished."

He followed his men out into the warehouse. Running footsteps echoed back to the prisoners.

Then came the crackle of flames, quickly building to a roar!

15 Hot Times

Wisps of smoke began filtering through the open doorway into the warehouse. Frank Hardy knew they'd just be the vanguard of what would come pouring through in seconds.

With his wrists and ankles bound, he wriggled like a snake toward the warehouse doorway. Frank twisted on the floor, managing to hook his feet behind the door. One good heave, and the door began to move. Then he could kick at the heavy metal panel until it swung shut.

"Good," Joe said, pushing himself to a sitting position. "I've breathed enough smoke this week."

"That was our only way out!" Kev Wylie's voice was shrill with fear. "You've locked us in!"

"We wouldn't last two minutes out there, tied up

like this," Russell Gilliam said. "At least we won't die of smoke inhalation."

"No, we just sit in here till we roast." From the sound of his voice, Kev had gone from hysterical to hopeless.

"We still have a chance," Frank replied sharply. "If we can get loose from these ropes—"

"Maybe I can help with that." Tom Gilliam scooted round, digging into his right back pocket. "In here—there's a box cutter—"

"Where did you get—" Russ Gilliam groaned in pain from his injured arm as Tom tried to cut through his father's bonds.

"Let me help." Joe inched toward Tom as quickly as he could.

"Those big guys stashed me in the warehouse, then waited to jump my dad." Tom skidded his way toward Joe. "While they were busy with him, I managed to slip a cutter into my pocket."

"Glad to hear you weren't carrying it in school." Joe reached Tom. "That's contraband."

Tom passed him the cutter. Then Joe began sawing at the other boy's wrists. It wasn't easy, working with his hands behind his back.

"Not much use against gangsters with guns," Tom said. "But now—that did it!"

The last strands of rope parted under the cutter. Tom took the blade and quickly sliced through Joe's wrist bonds.

Then he turned to his dad while Joe attacked the knots around his ankles.

Russ Gilliam sighed as his hands were freed. "I got a call as soon as I got home this evening," he said. "The meet was supposed to be in this office, but they were waiting for me in the warehouse." He glanced at Tom. "At least some good came of it."

Tom slashed his ankles free and went to cut Frank loose. Then he went to Don Wylie.

As soon as his hands were free, the businessman pulled the gag from his mouth. "We've got to get out of here before the whole place goes up!"

"Which will be all too soon." Frank was the closest to the door. He could feel the heat coming through. Even though they were now free, there was no hope of running for freedom that way. The whole warehouse was fully ablaze.

Getting to his feet, Frank scanned the room where they were trapped. This was a working office, not designed to impress. There were three metal desks and dozens of tall file cabinets. One door led to the warehouse. Another door—locked and with its knob smashed—led outside. That was hopeless.

And then there was a single, dusty, sealed window . . .

The inside was covered with a steel grating. Peering through the dirty glass, Frank could make out bars along the outside.

"This looks like the best way out," he said.

"Yeah, if we could drive a truck through it." Kev stared at the heavy metal fittings.

"So we'll have to make do with the next-best thing." Frank began slamming shut the open, gasoline-reeking drawers on one of the file cabinets.

Joe joined him, helping to manhandle the metal box across the floor.

"It's at moments like this that I remember that paper is made from trees." Joe grunted as he pushed against the steel casing. "You think maybe we should dump some of these files?"

"If we're going to use this as a battering ram, we'll need all the weight we can handle," Frank replied, a little breathless.

Now the others caught on. Kev and Don Wylie leaped to assist. So did Tom. Russ Gilliam, favoring his hurt arm, braced a shoulder behind the cabinet and pushed.

Screeching across the old linoleum floor, the four-drawer file nearly flew to the window.

"Turn it so the drawers will be on top when we pick it up," Frank ordered.

Frank set a foot against the back of the cabinet. Russ Gilliam heaved at the top. Four sets of hands stood ready to take the weight as the cabinet angled back, back . . .

"We've got the top!" Joe shouted from where he and Kev struggled for a hold.

"Here comes the bottom!" Don Wylie grunted

with effort as he and Tom fought to pick up the weight. Frank scrambled to help them. Now they had the file cabinet parallel with the floor.

"We'll all have to move together," Frank warned. "Okay, on my count. One step back . . . two steps . . ."

They staggered back under the weight of their makeshift battering ram.

"Now—charge!"

Desperately, they ran across the room. The top of the cabinet smashed against the grating and bounced back.

"Careful!" Joe yelled as the battering ram nearly leaped from their arms.

"Back up again!" Frank ordered. "Here we go! One step . . . two . . ."

As they repeated the moves, the teamwork became smoother. Two more thumps into the grating tore it free.

Success almost turned to disaster. The metal grillwork fell down on Joe and Kev as they pulled the file cabinet back.

"Let it go!" Frank shouted. "Get your hands out from under!"

The file cabinet fell to the floor with a deafening crash. For a second, they couldn't hear the noise of the flames in the warehouse.

With only one usable arm, Russ Gilliam hadn't been much help swinging the battering ram. But now he attacked the safety glass of the window with the heavy hammer Nicolai had left.

Joe joined him, battering the wire-reinforced glass out of its fittings. Then they made sure that no sharp shards were in the way for the attack on the outside window bars.

It was harder raising the file cabinet from where it lay flat on the floor. But working like madmen, they managed to lever the heavy weight up. Then, bracing themselves, they heaved, and heaved again. . . .

With an unearthly screech, the metal rods began parting company with the concrete they'd been set in. Sirens of arriving fire trucks added a weird harmony.

Firefighters were leaping off almost before the trucks came to a stop. Some ran to the warehouse entrance. Others dragged hoses and attaching them to the hydrants by the street. Gauntleted fists thundered against the office door.

"Anyone inside?" a voice called.

"Over here!" Frank yelled. "We're locked inside!"

Firefighters swarmed to the window as the bars finally popped free. Working feverishly with the newcomers, Frank and the others managed to bend the bars back, back . . .

At last, there was enough room for those inside to wriggle free.

The first one out was the still-unconscious guard. As Frank gently passed him into the waiting arms of the firefighters, he stared at the swollen lump on the man's skull.

Frank was the last out of the window. Behind him, a horrible red glow glared from all around the closed door into the warehouse. Smoke was filling the room. Frank coughed as he scrambled out and was caught by practiced hands.

Firefighters deposited him on the sidewalk outside the warehouse. A pair of arms supported him while a surprisingly pretty firefighter pressed a mask to Frank's face.

Oxygen-rich air poured into Frank's nose and mouth. Gently, the firefighter led him over to the trucks. An ambulance had arrived at some point. Frank had completely missed it.

"You were in the longest," the young woman said. "The paramedics will want to check you out."

An earth-shattering crash cut off her soothing words. Frank turned to see part of the warehouse roof fall in. Flames reared up through the hole, rising several stories into the sky.

On the ground firefighters redirected several of their hoses. Water arced through the air, landing on the roof around the hole.

Frank shook his head. The place looked like a complete loss. He hoped Don Wylie had been prudent with his insurance.

Wiping an arm across his stinging eyes, Frank took in the scene around him. Where was Mr. Wylie?

After a moment Frank found the businessman standing by a police car. Wylie was talking very intently with a patrol officer, who held up his mobile radio.

Even as Frank watched, another police car made its way through the chaos. Con Riley emerged and made a beeline for Donald Wylie.

Sure, Frank thought. If Kev's dad was guilty before, he'll be angry after Nicolai's attempted barbecue. Con will be getting an earful about Nicolai, his gang, and their plans.

Frank sighed, suddenly spotting Kev. The boy stood off to one side of the patrol car, watching his father. Did it help to see his father doing the right thing? Frank hoped so. Kev's whole world had been turned on its head this evening. He had really looked up to his dad. His confidence and trust had been severely shaken by Don Wylie's confessions.

Frank let himself be led off for his medical check. Speaking of fathers and sons . . .

Russ and Tom Gilliam stood by the ambulance. The older Gilliam had gotten a new sling for his arm. And off to one side was Joe, taking a sip from a cup.

"You okay?" Joe asked, taking in the air tank and mask.

"Fine." Frank didn't even cough as he answered. "I wonder if I could get hold of one of these gizmos for Bannerman's class."

Joe looked baffled.

"Believe me, sometimes you could use a shot of fresh air when he begins lecturing."

Joe was laughing as Tom and his dad came over.

"I have to thank you for getting us out of—that." Russ Gilliam's face was serious as he nodded to the burning warehouse. Yet, somehow, he looked much younger all of a sudden.

"We all worked together," Frank said. "And we got some crucial help from Tom and his trusty box cutter."

Tom chuckled, then got more serious. "Maybe this seems like a weird time to say it, but about that project"—he cleared his throat—"I'm not going to be captain."

"Are you off again?" Joe asked.

"No, we'll be in Bayport for a bit. Dad has some stuff he needs to straighten out. But I'm not going to make any arguments against whistle-blowing." Tom glanced at his father. "Not anymore."

"I'll talk to Phil and the other kids," Frank said. "I'm sure we can find another way to approach the project."

"If there's any help I can give," Russ Gilliam offered, "I'll happily talk about my former profession."

"Former?" Frank repeated.

The older man nodded. "If it sounds drastic, well, I had some drastic thinking to do when Tom disappeared. I realized—almost too late—that it was time to stop whistle-blowing and become a father."

He put his good arm around his son's shoulders. "There's a lot to sort out. But I have a financial cushion to do that. I'll set up a nice, quiet accounting business. A town where no one knows me . . ."

He turned away as a camera crew came charging out of a news van. "Which lets out Bayport, I'm afraid."

Frank nodded. "Do you think you'll miss digging up trouble?"

Gilliam watched the roaring flames consume the warehouse. "There's such a thing as getting out while you're ahead. I think Tom and I will have challenges enough, trying to settle down and be a family."

"I'll give it my best shot," Tom promised. "From now on Trouble Boy is history."

Frank laughed at Russ Gilliam's reply.

"That goes double for me, son," he said. "That goes double for me."

**Do your younger brothers and sisters
want to read books like yours?**

**Let them know there
are books just for *them!***

They can join Nancy Drew and her best
friends as they collect clues and solve
mysteries in

THE

NANCY DREW

NOTEBOOKS®

Starting with

#1 The Slumber Party Secret

#2 The Lost Locket

#3 The Secret Santa

#4 Bad Day for Ballet

AND

**Meet up with suspense and mystery
in The Hardy Boys® are: The Clues Brothers™**

Starting with

#1 The Gross Ghost Mystery

#2 The Karate Clue

#3 First Day, Worst Day

#4 Jump Shot Detectives

A MINSTREL® BOOK

Published by Pocket Books

BILL WALLACE

Award-winning author Bill Wallace brings you fun-filled
animal stories full of humor and exciting adventures.

A MINSTREL® BOOK

Published by Pocket Books

648-32

Todd Strasser's
AGAINST THE ODDS ™

Shark Bite

The sailboat is sinking, and Ian just saw the biggest shark of his life.

Grizzly Attack

They're trapped in the Alaskan wilderness with no way out.

Buzzard's Feast

Danger in the desert!

Gator Prey

They know the gators are coming for them...it's only a matter of time.

A MINSTREL® BOOK
Published by Pocket Books

2023